MISSION RECOVERY
"SPECIAL OPERATIONS"

Director: Thomas Casey
Deputy Director: Lucas Camp

When all else fails,
a Specialist is called in to "recover" a situation.

This team of highly skilled men and women was created to serve the needs of all other U.S. government agencies whenever the usual channels failed. The elite force is trained in every area of antiterrorism and aggressive infiltration. All agents have extensive stealth and sniper training and are multilingual. They must meet the most stringent mental and physical requirements of any national or international security force. They are prepared to do *whatever* it takes to accomplish their mission....

Failure is *not* an option.

SAFE HAVEN

DEBRA WEBB

Her Hidden Truth

HARLEQUIN®

TORONTO • NEW YORK • LONDON
AMSTERDAM • PARIS • SYDNEY • HAMBURG
STOCKHOLM • ATHENS • TOKYO • MILAN • MADRID
PRAGUE • WARSAW • BUDAPEST • AUCKLAND

ISBN-13: 978-0-373-36201-1
ISBN-10:   0-373-36201-3

HER HIDDEN TRUTH

DEBRA WEBB

Debra Webb was born in Scottsboro, Alabama, to parents who taught her that anything is possible if you want it bad enough. She began writing at age nine. Eventually, she met and married the man of her dreams, and tried some other occupations, including selling vacuum cleaners, working in a factory, a daycare center, a hospital and a department store. When her husband joined the military, they moved to Berlin, Germany, and Debra became a secretary in the commanding general's office. By 1985 they were back in the States, and finally moved to Tennessee, to a small town where everyone knows everyone else. With the support of her husband and two beautiful daughters, Debra took up writing again, looking to mystery and movies for inspiration. In 1998, her dream of writing for Harlequin Books came true. You can write to Debra with your comments at P.O. Box 64, Huntland, Tennessee 37345, or visit her Web site at www.debrawebb.com to find out exciting news about her next book.

This book is dedicated to all the wonderful readers who have taken the time out of their busy schedules to read my stories. Thank you so much for the opportunity to entertain you. Thanks for all your support.

Chapter One

Vincent Ferrelli rarely went looking for trouble, but somehow it always found him. Maybe it was the Harley he rode or maybe it was just the handsome face God had blessed or, depending upon the way one looked at it, cursed him with. Whatever the case, Vince never backed down from a challenge, personal or professional.

Never.

Those damned flyboys from Langley Air Force Base didn't know who they were messing with. Not one of the three—or all three together, for that matter—stood a chance in hell against an Italian boy born and street schooled in Trenton, New Jersey.

Oh, well, Vince mused, it was their funeral.

"Maybe you'd like to step outside and put your money where your mouth is," the tallest of the three, and the one who appeared to be the leader, suggested.

There was no way to know the guy's rank since he was dressed in civvies. But judging by his age, twenty-two or twenty-three, and the "wings" he'd boasted about, a first lieutenant maybe. Had probably just gotten those wings and thought he could rule the world. The other two were most likely from the same class. Fresh out of fighter-pilot training and ready to play the Air Force version of *Top Gun*.

But not tonight.

"It'd be my pleasure," Vince said, barely restraining a grin as adrenaline raced through his veins. This would be a piece of cake. Casey would have his ass come morning, but tonight Vince was going to show these guys that you didn't need wings or a buzz cut to be bad.

On more than one occasion Vince had been told that he was bad...bad to the bone. And why not? He'd earned it. A former U.S. Navy SEAL and now a Specialist in the most highly covert government agency.

Hell, yeah, he was bad.

And in the mood to blow off a little steam.

Vince followed the three outside the Lady Liberty Lounge. A blast of rock music tagged along but was quickly muffled by the door closing behind them. The still, sticky air hung in the July night like a shimmering ghost.

There were two things a guy could count on after dark during a D.C. summer, thickening humidity and restlessness. This part of the city literally vibrated at night—came to life in a way that was both alluring and dangerous. His own boredom had drawn Vince out to this sleazebag joint tonight. The need to do anything but watch another episode of some sitcom. The primal urge to discover the secrets the night held.

He should have stayed home.

If he had stayed home he wouldn't be about to trade punches with these lightweights. There was nothing Vince hated more than waiting for his next mission. This time was going to prove no exception. And this time the trouble he usually attempted to avoid had found him.

The dim streetlights barely cut through the darkness, lending just enough illumination to get a readout on the facial expressions and body language of his opponents. The parking lot was jam-packed with the cars of patrons, but completely empty of people. They were all inside, gyrating to classic rock music, staking claims and pumping up the sexual tension. There would be no one to witness the lesson he was about to teach these still-wet-behind-the-ears gentlemen.

That was probably a good thing.

The biggest and beefiest of the three stepped forward. The way his nose crooked to the left, it was pretty clear that he was no stranger to barroom brawls.

"I tell you what, old man," he said smugly, "just to even up the odds, why don't you and I go one-on-one and the winner can take it from there."

Okay, so he'd seen thirty his last birthday. That didn't make him old by any stretch of the imagination. Vince shrugged in response, not even bothering to justify the ridiculous comment. Instead he took a moment to survey the spiffy, well-polished group. He'd bet a big, sweet slice of his mom's cherry pie that every part of their wardrobe, down to the skivvies, sported designer labels purchased straight from the Post Exchange. These guys were green in every sense of the word.

When Vince had looked his fill, he said, "Makes no difference to me, *boys.*"

Fury claimed the beefy guy's expression. "I'm gonna enjoy wiping that grin off your face," he threatened.

"Take your best shot," Vince offered as he motioned with both hands for the guy to come and get him. Might as well get this over with so he could get back to the beer he'd left at the bar, along with the sexy blonde who'd deserted these flyboys in favor of Vince, which was the whole reason this little war had started. Just another reason Vince should have stayed home tonight. He'd been dwelling on the past again…a sure sign he wasn't thinking straight.

Before the muscled gorilla could make his first move a car skidded to a stop right behind Vince. Careful to keep most of his attention on the threesome ready to take off his head, Vince glanced over his shoulder. The sight of a long, black limousine confused him at first, then a window powered down.

His boss. Director Thomas Casey.

Great. Just great.

"Get in the car," Casey ordered. He did not look happy.

"We have unfinished business with him," the beefy guy bellowed, impatient, belligerent. "He's not going no place until we're through."

The three started to close in on Vince. He was just about to tell Casey he'd only be a minute when the sound of Lucas Camp's voice stopped him.

"Back off," Lucas commanded. "I'd hate to have to use this."

Fully expecting to find Lucas wielding a weapon, Vince looked across the top of the automobile at his direct supervisor, the Deputy Director of Mission Recovery. To his surprise Lucas held a mere cellular phone in his right hand.

"I'm sure General Fielding would be less than pleased to be awakened at this time of night for such a petty nuisance. And since he's a personal friend of mine, I'm even more certain he'd be happy to see that you gentlemen were immediately transferred to Minot."

Silence ruled the night for about five seconds.

"We're all through here, sir," the tallest man said quickly, obviously not willing to risk being shipped to the middle of nowhere in North Dakota. He pushed in front of his brawny friend and shook his head at the guy. "We have an early call to formation in the morning."

Vince blew out an exasperated breath as the three men headed back into the bar without so much as a fleeting glance in his direction. "Two minutes tops," he griped to Lucas. "That's all I needed. You couldn't wait two minutes."

"Get in the car, Ferrelli," Lucas growled.

His annoyance rising as the adrenaline receded, Vince reluctantly obeyed the order. He knew better than to push it. "What's up?" he asked as soon as he'd settled into the seat across from the top brass of Mission Recovery. The limo rolled into forward motion without preamble. Vince would have to come back for his Harley when the impromptu meeting was over. Anticipation kicked in. It had to be important for them to look him up this time of night.

"We have a mission for you," Casey explained. "You'll need to leave first thing in the morning."

Since it was practically morning already, Vince decided that was fine with him. At least he wouldn't have to pace the floors of his tiny apartment any longer. He had a mission. About time.

"I'm ready. What's the job?"

"The CIA has an operative in trouble," Lucas told him. "She's been under deep cover for one month now. She's infiltrated a small group of extremists who think they're working for the World Security Agency."

Vince frowned, searching for any recognition. He found none. "The World Security Agency?"

"Doesn't exist," Lucas explained.

Casey took over from there. "The CIA has been tracking the so-called WSA for almost a year now. They recruit young people across the nation to support their cause by assuring them that they're doing their patriotic duty. So far WSA has been successful twice."

"The bombing at LAX six months ago," Lucas interjected, "and the attempt on the United Nations building just two months ago. Four or five are usually recruited and all of them die when the mission is completed, successful or not."

"How did the CIA manage to get someone inside?" Vince wanted to know. If all leads wound up dead ends, the CIA had done a pretty good trick by getting someone inside.

"One guy survived the UN attack," Lucas went on. "Philip Yu. The CIA has been tracking him since. We don't know why he was allowed to live and the others were killed, but it was a lucky break."

"So the CIA sent someone in to get close to Yu?" Vince suggested.

"Right. Yu had already recruited three others before the CIA's operative. If the same modus operandi prevails, we believe they'll attempt something soon. We don't have much time."

"And you're going to let it play out in hopes of nabbing the brains behind the operation," Vince finished for him. It wasn't a question. Sounded like his kind of mission.

Lucas nodded. "We'll never stop them if we don't cut off the head of the organization."

"Cool." Vince considered the one thing that didn't add up. "Why isn't the FBI running lead on this?" The whole scenario spelled Bureau jurisdiction to him.

"They were," Casey said. "Until intelligence pointed to a David Kovner as one of the top echelon of WSA."

"Israeli?"

Casey nodded affirmatively to Vince's question. "The CIA took over from there. As well as being dangerous, this guy is a huge embarrassment to our Israeli friends. They want him stopped, but they need our help to finish the job."

"So who am I and where am I going?"

Lucas and Casey exchanged a look. The tension started in Vince's gut, but swiftly worked its way up his back to his shoulders. He didn't like that look. It could only mean trouble right up front.

In this business, starting off on the wrong foot or one step behind could be a very bad thing.

"Port Charlotte, Virginia," Lucas said in answer to his second question. "It's a college town off Highway 1 between Woodbridge and Fredericksburg. Yu and his team share a large rental house there. Three of the group are enrolled in the university. In their spare time they've been training in the art of surgical demolitions. We know how Yu is getting his orders. We just can't catch Kovner in the act. We need to tie him to WSA."

Vince wasn't the top demo expert in Mission Recovery but he was pretty damned good. There had to be some other reason he'd been chosen. His director's next words told him the question was written on his face.

"We selected you for this mission," Casey told him in answer to his unspoken inquiry, "because we need your particular multilingual skills in the event it becomes an issue and we need someone who can handle the demo aspect of the assignment."

Vince was fluent in seven languages. But he knew that wasn't the only reason he'd been chosen. All Specialists were multilingual. The tension radiating between the two men seated across from him was too intense for it to be so simple.

"The CIA operative involved is the first to field test a new memory implant," Lucas went on. "The purpose of the implant is to keep an operative out of trouble if the cover is in jeopardy. When the implant is activated the operative's own memory is suppressed and effectively replaced by the cover profile in the implant. Nothing, not drugs or torture, will induce the operative into confessing, since he or she becomes the cover profile."

"That's a new one." Vince was familiar with the CIA's reputation for experimental projects. "So when the implant is activated, the Company knows the operative is in jeopardy?" Vince also knew that CIA operatives were closely monitored. They'd been using tracking devices for years now.

Lucas nodded. "Since this is the first time they've even had a lead on this so-called World Security Agency, they don't want to lose this operative. If the mission is salvageable, they want it completed. But if it's not, your job is to try to get the operative out safely. The implant, if functioning properly, is only temporary. Time is very short."

Vince nodded his understanding. "Sounds easy enough. Tell me about the operative."

"Katrina Moore. Age twenty-seven." Lucas ticked off the details. "She's been with the Company since being rejected by the SEALs four years ago."

Kat. Things went very quiet inside Vince as the memories from four years ago came flooding back on a tidal wave. Conflicting emotions tugged at him... renewed the regret that never really went away.

"The two of you have a history?" Casey said, no doubt reading Vince's startled expression or somehow having prior knowledge. But that was impossible. No one knew...

Hesitant to admit something so intensely private, Vince finally nodded once. "Yeah, kind of. I was one of her instructors in BUDS." Both men knew that BUDS— Basic Underwater Demolition SEALs—was the most rigorous personnel training outfit in the Navy.

"Which she failed," Lucas remarked.

Failed wasn't the right word. Kat had been doomed from the word go. The elite Navy SEALs didn't want women among their ranks. No matter if she was good enough. Kat was as good as any of the men, better than some, but that fact hadn't changed the bottom line. The powers that be had drummed up an acceptable reason to performance drop her and it was done. She'd felt betrayed when she hadn't made the cut.

She'd felt betrayed by Vince.

And rightly so. Though his vote alone wouldn't have made any real difference in the end, he'd caved and followed the antiquated rules. He'd voted against her...despite what he thought...despite what they'd shared.

"Yeah," he said in answer to Lucas's prodding. "But it wasn't because she wasn't good enough," he clarified quickly. "She was a woman. That was the only reason."

"Do you think she holds that failure against you?" Casey asked.

"Not entirely," he admitted after a tense moment. "She knows it was not my decision alone." He looked Casey straight in the eye. "But she has other reasons to resent me that are far more personal than that."

Lucas laughed, but the sound held no humor. "The two of you had a thing going during training and you betrayed her?" He shook his head. "Son, haven't you ever heard of the term 'fraternization'? They could have hung you for that. She could have ruined your career."

But she hadn't. The cold reality of that truth sank all the way to Vince's bones. She could have had her revenge. What he'd done had been wrong in more ways than one. He'd disgraced himself, whether anyone else ever knew it or not—had allowed a weakness. For that reason he had walked away from his hard-earned career. Because he hadn't been worthy of it any longer.

A full year later Lucas Camp had knocked on his door and offered him a way to redeem himself professionally. But nothing had assuaged his conscience where Kat was concerned. There had been no way to make that right.

Until now…maybe.

"That's right," he snapped. "I screwed her over and she hated me for it." He swallowed, the effort difficult. Those demons haunted him…made him regret a great deal more than either of their failed career moves. "I can't say that I blame her, but it's done. I can't change it now. And she didn't have to end my career. I made an unforgivable mistake. I resigned because of it."

"So your personal reasons for leaving your military career were more personal than you led us to believe. This should make things interesting," Lucas said as he flipped through what was probably Kat's file.

"Maybe you'd better pick someone else for this assignment," Vince suggested tightly. "Not that I don't want to do it, but Kat—Miss Moore—might be more receptive to someone else. My presence might actually put her in more jeopardy. I don't want that." He wouldn't do anything that might hurt her. No way.

"That's not possible," Lucas said succinctly.

The tension in Vince's gut ratcheted up another notch or two. "Why not?" he asked—demanded actually. "Sending me in could be a big mistake."

"There's a back door built into the implant," Lucas explained grimly. "For this very scenario. To facilitate a retrieval, the implant was designed with what the Company calls a *Romeo* option. All you have to do is say the code phrase and Katrina will instantly recognize you as the lover with whom she's still involved."

Vince held out both hands stop-sign fashion. "Wait just a minute." He dropped his hands and exhaled a heavy breath. "I'm telling you the woman hates me. I don't think any implant is going to change that deeply ingrained emotion. The second she sees my face, the mission will be blown all to hell."

Lucas pointed a no-arguments look in Vince's direction. "Maybe she does hate you. But that's neither here nor there, Ferrelli. The fact of the matter is that she used you for her Romeo profile. You're the *only* man for this mission. If Katrina Moore was willing to bet her life on you, then who are we to dispute the issue?"

Vince felt stunned.

Lucas leaned forward slightly when Vince remained speechless. "She described you down to the very last detail." He lifted a skeptical eyebrow. "I think maybe her memory was a little dim in some areas."

Vince didn't find any of it amusing. His concern for Kat's safety mushroomed in tandem with his dread, but he didn't ask a single question while Lucas rattled off the rest of the details of the mission. The whole thing felt like a dream…not necessarily a bad dream, but one that made him extremely uneasy.

Payback, Vince decided. It couldn't be anything else. A second or two later his mind had wrapped fully around the concept. It was the perfect chance for Kat to get even with him. A part of him wanted to think otherwise, but he knew better. He'd hurt her too badly. He would never forget the look in those big green eyes when she learned that she'd been performance dropped from the graduating class for no real reason.

She'd left and he hadn't seen her since. But he'd thought about her now and then…and every moment in between.

He'd thought about her every day for four years, but he'd stopped trying to keep tabs on her after she joined the Company, the revered CIA.

One way or another he wouldn't let her down this time.

NEARLY AN HOUR LATER the limo braked to a stop next to Vince's Harley in the parking lot of the Lady Liberty Lounge. The place was still jumping, the lot still overflowing and the music thumping all the louder through the thin exterior walls. Vince wondered vaguely if the blonde had made up with her flyboys.

In the last fifty minutes they'd discussed one-by-one the team members with whom Kat was involved. Vince now had a clear mental picture of each. Only one, Philip Yu himself, worried Vince.

"Any questions?" Lucas asked, studying Vince closely. The guy was way too smart and read people far too easily. Lucas recognized that Vince had a real problem with this mission, but he'd do what he had to.

Retrieving Kat was priority one. Though, technically, salvaging the mission was supposed to be his first goal, this one was personal. Even Casey had to see that. They couldn't expect anything else under the circumstances. Casey didn't have to say it and he wouldn't. Thomas Casey was a man of few words. No one really knew him, except maybe Lucas.

"I think I've got it." Vince reached for the door handle. He'd pack and get on the road before dawn. He wanted to see firsthand as soon as possible that Kat was safe.

"Don't try to intercept the target until she's alone," Casey suggested. "We have no way of knowing her status. She may fully believe she's the enemy she was assigned to infiltrate. That would be the best case scenario. If," he went on grimly, "the implant has malfunctioned and the code doesn't trigger the right response, you could be putting yourself in serious jeopardy."

Vince met that intense blue gaze. "I won't approach while she's with the others unless there's no other window of opportunity."

Casey dipped his head in acknowledgment. "If too much risk is involved, back off. We'll send in an entire team. The CIA won't like it, but they'll live with it."

"Yes, sir." Vince nodded to Lucas then climbed out of the vehicle. Before turning away he tapped on the closed window, then waited for it to power down to reveal Lucas's expectant expression. "Who's got my back on this one?" Vince asked, just now remembering that he should. Of course, the information would be in the mission profile.

"Callahan."

Perfect. Blue Callahan was the best sharp shooter in the bunch—even if she was a girl. Vince couldn't help smiling at the irony of the situation.

"That's great," he said to Lucas.

"Glad you approve." Lucas started to power up the window but hesitated. "Not that it would have made any difference," he added pointedly before sending the darkly tinted window the rest of the way up.

Vince watched as the limousine disappeared down the next block. Lucas Camp was easy to work for. He was straight up and in your face. The director was another story. Vince would never understand Thomas Casey. Just when he thought he had the guy figured out, he goes and says something totally out of character. As though he really cared about the people who worked for him or something.

Maybe he did. Then again, maybe he just didn't want to look bad to the Company hotshots breathing down his neck on this one.

Shaking his head, Vince straddled his Harley. He inserted the key and gave it a quick flick. The perfectly tuned engine roared to life. He could spend a lifetime studying a guy like Casey and never understand what made him tick. But right now he had something much more important to do.

He had to get close to Kat. Had to keep her safe. Even if she didn't want him to.

If she did accept him, it would only be the implant, not the real Kat, he reminded himself. The real Kat had most likely forgotten all about him long ago.

Vince released the clutch and rocketed toward the street. She might have forgotten, but he would never forget.

Chapter Two

The headache was worse today.

Kat squeezed her eyes shut and tried to banish the pain, but it just wouldn't go away. She couldn't remember when it had begun…days ago…a week? It just kept getting worse. The bouts closer together. More intense.

Forcing her eyes open, she stared at her reflection in the bathroom mirror. Aspirin didn't help. Nothing helped. She blew out a long, slow breath. She had to pull it together. In three minutes she had to be ready to perform.

Kat splashed some cool water on her face in the hope of clearing the haze that accompanied the insistent pounding in her brain. That attempt proved useless, as well. She groped blindly for a paper towel. The holder was empty. She muttered her favorite swearword and wiped the moisture from her face the best she could with the backs of her hands. That was the thing about public bathrooms. One could never count on the necessary paper to finish the job.

Turning her head side to side to check the neatly coiled

bun, Kat tucked a stray, fiery red curl behind her ear and smoothed her moist palms over her hair. She studied herself a moment longer than necessary, something about the person staring back at her didn't sit exactly right, but she couldn't put her finger on the problem.

Kat shrugged. Nothing she could do about that, either. She looked herself over again, then, satisfied with what she saw, slipped on the large, black-framed eyeglasses that were part of her disguise. She slid a hand over the jacket of her gray business suit, finding comfort in the tiny bulge in the waistband of her skirt that was for emergency use only. She preferred a 9 mm, but the .38 proved easier to conceal.

No one was supposed to die today.

Still, she wasn't about to go into this without a way to defend herself if things went to hell in a hurry. And that could happen. Another of those things she somehow understood without knowing how.

Inhaling, then exhaling another bolstering breath, Kat picked up her brown leather briefcase and left the inadequately supplied ladies' room.

Two minutes and counting.

At a quarter of noon, Union Station was crowded. She'd taken the time this morning as she entered D.C.'s famous train gateway to the capital to note the neoclassical facade. Inside the cavernous marble-floored lobby she'd felt the rumble of the trains below as they entered the station. It was all so familiar…comforting. She felt at home here but she had no clue why. Had she lived near here in the past? Been a regular commuter? She shook her head. She was being silly. A person remembered the places she'd lived. Paranoia, that's all. She was just being paranoid.

The sound of the announcer singing out the track and time for the next Metroliner jerked her attention back to the task at hand. Some part of her that she didn't understand and that was pure, well-honed survival instinct, kept the pain at bay as she focused on what had to be done. She just pushed through the throng of hurrying commuters and toward the down escalator.

Though she couldn't name any precise instances at the moment, she'd done this sort of thing for years. She knew it as well as she knew her name, but wasn't exactly sure how she knew. Kat was completely at ease with tracking a human target. She'd done it a thousand times. The basis of that fact also eluded her. It simply felt second nature.

God, what was wrong with her lately? She knew who and what she was…she just couldn't get right with it all. It was as if a brick wall stood between her and the answers she desperately needed. It was weird.

Too weird.

But, like the headaches, she couldn't think about that right now. She damn sure couldn't let any of her cohorts see her inner struggle. Too many of them already wanted her out. Regrettably, out was synonymous with dead.

Her target moved toward the loading platform where he would catch the Metroliner to New York's Penn Station. Kat closed in. Once in Manhattan he would rendezvous with his superiors at the new CIA branch office. In his briefcase he carried documents that would mislead those who interpreted them and cause a very important ongoing mission to blow up in their faces.

Kat had to prevent that from happening.

She was a good guy. One of her country's invisible saviors. Countries all over the globe had them…all commissioned by the World Security Agency.

The world's savior.

A frown inched across her brow as something deep inside her shifted, nudged her. As everything else, she couldn't name it or understand it.

The man in the blue pin-striped suit standing only a dozen feet from Kat was no bad guy himself. He had no idea that his assistant was a mole for one of the CIA's archenemies. It was Kat's job to intercept the intelligence documents in the briefcase, thus preventing the planned catastrophe without any bloodshed or violence at all. Before the mole could arrange a second attempt he would be discovered and dealt with accordingly.

The briefcase Kat carried was an exact duplicate of the one her target carried. Expensive, elegant. Just like the thousand-dollar suit he wore. Kat watched the man's body language. He was confident, impatient. In a hurry to get to his destination and get this done. Failure would be a disappointment not only to his superiors but also to him. But he'd get over it. Eventually he'd look back on today as nothing more than a temporary setback to his career.

Kat had just ninety seconds to make the switch before he boarded the arriving passenger train.

A screeching, hissing rush of air that seemed to fill the entire waiting area announced the train's arrival as it slowed to a stop at the loading platform. In seconds the waiting passengers would be allowed to board.

She had to move now.

Bracing herself for the impact, Kat began to walk faster. Faster. She slammed headlong into her target. He stumbled back several steps, the briefcase in his hand falling to the floor. Kat dropped her own case as she used his tall frame to regain her balance.

"Oh, I'm so sorry!" she cried.

He reached to steady her—chivalry too deeply entrenched to ignore, despite his years of training—and at the same time demanded, "Are you all right?"

Kat smiled engagingly as she played the part of the flustered, in-a-hurry passenger. "Oh, yes. I'm…I'm fine." She reached for the briefcase, tracing one fingertip over the lock mechanism to make sure she had his instead of her own. The locking mechanism of the briefcase she'd carried had a slight burr in the metal in a certain spot so she'd recognize it. "I wasn't watching where I was going. I'm so late!" She eased back just one step and pressed a hand to her chest as if to slow her palpitating heart. "I am so very sorry."

His answering smile told her he didn't suspect a thing. "No harm done." He straightened his jacket and reached for the remaining briefcase. "Have a nice day."

For one tension-filled second, before she turned away, he stared at the briefcase she held half hidden behind her short skirt. She hoped her legs would distract him.

Her heart skidded to a stop as time lapsed into slow motion.

She held her breath.

If he suspected her now—

The legs did the trick.

His gaze roved the length of her long, athletic limbs. She'd worked hard to keep them that way, and it was paying off now. The realization startled her for reasons that totally escaped her. A tremble started deep inside her. She was losing it…she had to get out of here.

Other passengers abruptly brushed past the man still staring at her, jerking him back to attention. He blinked, forced a grim smile and quickly turned away to board the train, a bemused frown still marring his brow.

Kat released a shaky breath.

It was done.

She hurried away through the crowd, taking care not to run. Up the escalator. Deep breath, she told herself. Almost there. No one paid any special note to her. No one shouted for her to stop.

She moved back through the lobby as swiftly as she dared. She couldn't risk calling attention to herself even now. Her target would attempt to open his briefcase the moment he took his seat onboard the train and had a chance to think about the encounter. He wouldn't rest until he'd assuaged the concerns that took root too late in his distracted thoughts.

The lock had been jammed so it would take some doing to open the case. By the time he realized what had happened, the train would be on its way. He would call

Union Station security immediately and the whole place would be locked down tighter than a drum. Her description would be passed to all Metro Security personnel.

She had to get out before that happened.

Her heart hammering, her palms sweating, her fingers tight around the handle of the briefcase, she hurried toward the main entrance. When she pushed through the wood-and-glass front doors and out into the bright noonday sun, relief flooded her, made her weak-kneed, despite the gut instinct that she'd done this hundreds of times.

She zigzagged through the taxis and other cars parked along the train terminal's busy driveway and headed toward the far end of the main parking area where the car she'd arrived in waited. Her step was a little faster now, not quite running.

Two more minutes and she'd be in the clear. A kind of calmness slid through her veins. Her heart rate slowed to a more reasonable level. She could—

A strong arm abruptly cut across her path, stopping her dead in her tracks. Her pulse leaped into warp speed again. Her somewhat sluggish reactions went automatically into offense mode.

Fully expecting to see a blue security uniform, she instinctively, stealthily, slid her hand toward the edge of her jacket lapel as she peered upward into smoky-gray eyes that were at once completely alien to her and alarmingly familiar.

"Well, well, if it isn't the love of my life."

Her fingers wrapped around the butt of the small .38.

"I've missed you, and then some."

For three gut-wrenching seconds Vince was certain the code phrase wasn't going to work. Kat stared up at him as if she'd never laid eyes on him in her entire life.

Then she whispered, "Vince?"

He relaxed a fraction and smiled. "Long time no see, Kitty Kat. Have you missed me, too?" Maybe the implant hadn't gone too haywire. He'd been watching her all morning. Had followed her all the way from Port Charlotte just to catch her alone. It shifted something deep inside him when he considered that she'd remembered that little thing he always said to her all those years ago. *I've missed you, and then some.*

"Don't move."

The voice was male and right behind Vince. The nudge of a pistol barrel in his spleen told him it was Kat's partner in crime, Philip Yu. The driver of the getaway car. Thankfully he'd stayed in the car and this opportunity had been the closest to catching Kat alone the morning had offered. Interrupting her assignment would have put them both at risk. Vince had tried to wait it out, but he'd had to act before she got back in the car with Yu. Now he'd learn the price of his impatience.

"You know this dude, Kat?"

She looked from Vince to the man behind him and back. The confusion on her face was clear to see. Tension rocketed to a new level. Maybe things weren't in working order, after all. He'd soon know.

"Phil, this is Vince." She searched Vince's eyes,

looking for answers he hoped she'd see. "He's the guy I've been telling you about."

The pressure in Vince's side eased. He resisted the urge to exhale his relief.

"The case," Yu demanded as he reached around Vince.

Kat relinquished her bounty. "We should get out of here," she suggested. She glanced behind her, then scanned the parking area. "They'll be looking for me any second now."

Yu backed away. "Let's go."

Vince turned in the other man's direction. "She goes with me."

Something changed in Yu's eyes. "I don't think so."

Lucas's intel was correct. Philip Yu had a thing for Kat. Too bad for him. Something that felt entirely too much like jealousy burned through Vince as he snaked an arm around her waist and pulled her close before she could react.

"Maybe you didn't hear me." Vince met the steel in Yu's dark gaze with lead in his own. This part was non-negotiable. "*I said* she goes with me."

"We'll be right behind you," Kat assured her partner. She glanced up at Vince. "Right?"

She was nervous. He could see it in her eyes. "That's right." He settled his gaze back on Yu's. "Are we going to stand around here and argue about it?"

Yu glared at Vince then shifted his gaze to Kat. "We'll talk about this later."

In typical Kat fashion, she ignored Yu's comment, pulled out of Vince's domineering hold and hooked her arm through his. "See you at the house," she said to Yu without even looking his way. She hated the macho male types. Vince would never understand what had drawn them together in the first place.

Yu hustled across the lot, tossed the briefcase into the passenger seat and dropped behind the wheel of the car he'd abandoned when he thought Kat was in trouble.

Vince looked down at the woman at his side. His gut clenched. God, she was gorgeous. She hadn't changed a bit. Not quite as lean maybe, but otherwise just as he remembered. That alone was far more dangerous than any other aspect of this mission.

"You ready?"

She nodded, her smile a little thin.

He led her to where he'd parked his Harley. After strad-dling the wide leather seat, he waited for her to join him. Without hesitation she scooted her skirt high on her thighs—high enough for him to see the sexy garters that held up her stockings—and slung one long, toned leg across the seat. She settled in behind him, then scooted even closer, her thighs clenching firmly around his hips as her arms curled tightly around his waist. As an afterthought she reached up and discarded her fake eyeglasses. She laughed. The sound was contagious and as sexy as hell.

Vince tried not to confuse the past with the present. He really did. Whatever memories her implant had transposed over her real memory, were only make-believe. No matter how real this felt, it wasn't. When she realized the truth she would hate him just as much, maybe more, than she had four years ago. That kind of emotion didn't sweeten with age, it grew bitter. Kat would be bitter, as she had every right to be.

He'd let her down—betrayed her.

But now he had one chance to make it up to her. A chance she would never give him under normal circumstances. He gritted his teeth against his own churning emotions. Changing her mind about him would be impossible, but he could keep her safe until this was over. No matter how little she thought of him, she would appreciate walking away from this assignment with her life. And that he could do for her.

She pressed her cheek against his back, an act of trust.

A new kind of emotion surged through him. A mixture of relief and anticipation. She trusted him, temporarily anyway.

This time he would not let her down.

At the moment he couldn't be sure what had made her use him as her Romeo. It didn't matter. Revenge, probably. A mistake maybe? He might never know the reason and it really didn't matter anyway.

In minutes they were on the interstate headed back to Port Charlotte. As if sensing that he was thinking of her, she hugged him more tightly. Unable to help himself, he laid his left hand over hers and squeezed. God, he hadn't known until now how much he'd missed this incredible woman. No one else had ever made him want to change his singular lifestyle. White picket fences and the pitter-patter of little feet had flashed, however briefly, through his mind during their days of stolen moments and hidden passion four years ago.

No other woman had made him want to see her face every morning for the rest of his life…made him ache to simply touch her the way Kat had. Had made him willingly turn his back on all that he'd considered top priority.

But that was then and this is now.

The object of his reverie suddenly tapped him on the shoulder, jerking him to attention. Vince leaned his head back to hear what she had to say. Instead of speaking, she pointed to an upcoming gas station. He nodded his understanding. She either wanted a drink or needed to use the facilities.

He desperately needed to walk off the tension she'd incited below his belt. Clearing his head with even a few seconds apart would help, as well.

The one bathroom offered by the old-fashioned, full-service gas station was on the right side of the building and all the way at the back. Vince checked out the four-by-four room before allowing Kat inside. It was cleaner than he'd expected. Apparently the old geezer who ran the fifties-style joint was a neatnik.

"Is the coast clear?" Kat teased. She leaned back against the wall next to the bathroom door. "I do have a gun, you know." She cocked one finely arched auburn eyebrow. "And I haven't forgotten how to use it."

Vince resisted the impulse to tell her everything. To ask her what she really remembered, but it would be a mistake. The implant was in control, that was obvious. She would have taken his head off by now otherwise. His mission was to play this out to see if he could finger the guy in charge of WSA. As long as continuing didn't endanger Kat's life, completing the mission was essential.

"Just making sure the facilities were fit for a princess," he returned just as playfully. They'd sparred like this all those years ago.

She pushed off the wall and sashayed into the bathroom. "I'll only be a minute," she said over her shoulder, her tone flirtatious, inviting.

Vince looked away as the door closed behind her. He had to regain his perspective here. It would be too easy to fall into the old routine of taking what she had to offer. What he desperately wanted.

Except it wouldn't be fair to Kat. She was not herself. Had no control over the situation. He'd been a jerk with her once. He wouldn't make the same mistake twice.

The door abruptly opened halfway. "I've got a little problem in here, Vince." She reached out and grabbed his sleeve. "You don't mind helping a girl out, now do you?" She tugged, pulling him to the door.

"What kind of problem?"

She had him in the room and the door closed behind him before the hesitant words were fully out of his mouth. Anticipation spiked, as did his male equipment. This was not a good thing.

Kat shoved him against the closed door and immediately started unbuttoning his shirt. "Why do you do this to me, Vinny?" she demanded petulantly.

No one had ever called him Vinny, except Kat. It touched him…but now wasn't the time. He manacled her hands and held them still. "We don't have time for this right now," he urged, his whole body hardening at the prospect she presented.

"You disappear for weeks, leaving me to my own devices." She looked up at him, those green eyes hooded, that luscious mouth puckered in a little pout. "Could get a girl in all kinds of trouble."

"Kat, you—"

"Shh," she purred, then tugged loose from his grasp and whispered, "I just can't be expected to wait a minute longer." She stood on tiptoes and brushed her lips against his.

All thought processes ceased. He couldn't breathe. Couldn't move. Damn sure couldn't speak with her looking at him that way…touching him that way.

Her fingers tangled with his buttons once more. "All you have to do is let me have my way." Her hungry mouth captured his in a demanding kiss.

He should have resisted. Should have pushed her away. But he simply didn't possess the strength to do it. His fingers found their way into her hair. He jerked the pins away until those silky auburn tresses fell around his hands. Her cool fingers moved over his chest sending a fire raging through him. She teased his nipples, making them bud and burn. Traced the ridges of his abdomen. Then tugged at the closure to his jeans.

Her wicked tongue thrust in and out of his mouth in time with the undulating of her hips against his rigid pelvis. He was coming unglued one piece at a time. He was hard as a rock. His mind was reeling and he couldn't touch her all the places he wanted to at once.

Her hair…the curve of her spine…the swell of her bottom. He lifted her more firmly against him. She moaned, the sound fueling the desire already out of control inside him.

She kissed him harder, then pulled free, her lips following the new path of her hands. Along his throat, over one aching nipple and downward. She teased him, dipping her tongue beneath his waistband, all the while squeezing his buttocks. Vince closed his eyes and told himself he could be stronger than this. Commanded himself to pull it together.

He couldn't do it.

He pulled her back into his arms, did a one-eighty turn and pressed her against the closed door. He kissed her the way he wanted to…the way he'd dreamed of kissing her for four long, lonely years. He hiked her skirt up to her waist and pushed hard between her welcoming thighs. Another throaty groan echoed in the room, whether from him or her, he couldn't say.

He found the spot that was hot and wet for him. Touched her there. He trembled. She did the same. She pulled free of the kiss and cried out his name, her fingers fisting in his shirt, tugging it from his jeans. He trembled again at the needy sound of her voice. He dragged a finger along that ultrasensitive place and reveled in her response. She arched her spine, offering that slick warmth for his taking.

"Please don't make me wait any longer," she murmured. Her eyes opened and she looked directly at him. "Please," she whimpered.

In those shimmering jade pools he saw his reflection. Saw the man who was prepared to hurt the only woman he'd ever cared about all over again.

He couldn't do it.

Not even to maintain his cover.

Chapter Three

There was definitely something very wrong with her. Even Vince rejected her. He'd never done *that* before. They had always taken any opportunity available to make love. Hadn't they? Uncertainty pulled in her stomach.

Kat went cold despite still being held firmly in his strong, warm embrace, her legs coiled around his lean waist.

"We should get going," Vince said in that husky baritone that always affected her far more deeply than she wanted to admit.

As she dropped her feet to the floor and pushed him away, she held that smoky gaze, searched for any little flicker that might reveal what was going through that handsome head of his. Before he'd said a single word, she had felt his emotional withdrawal. Felt it and denied it, until he'd articulated with actual words. Her chest tightened, sending a flood of too familiar emptiness through her.

He didn't want her.

Had he met someone else while he was away this time? Or was it simply something he found lacking in her? Maybe both.

Either way, it was a low blow.

Anger ignited inside her. "What's wrong? Having a slow week, Vinny?" She shoved her fingers through her hair, shaking loose the rest of the pins, then glared up at him. "Or maybe you're not yourself."

His pupils flared ever so slightly, as if she'd hit the nail on the head. His beard-shadowed jaw hardened like granite right in front of her eyes. "I don't want your new friend going ballistic because we're not right behind him."

She didn't miss the hint of jealousy in his tone. Good. It was only fair that they were both miserable. "You're right. I don't know what I was thinking."

Kat spun around and reached for the doorknob. She wanted to scream. She trusted Vince. Cared deeply for him. Why would he reject her? Something long buried stirred inside her, filled her with dread. The sensation startled her…scared her a little. She tightened her fingers on the knob, gave it a ruthless twist and jerked the door open.

She was out of here.

At first, recognition of the face staring down at her from the other side of the threshold didn't register. Kat instinctively reached for her weapon, but realization, a little slow in coming, stopped her.

Phil.

It was only Phil.

She swore. "You scared the hell out of me." She spat

the words, her glower every bit as fierce as the dark one focused her way.

Phil looked from Kat to Vince. "We don't have time for *this*." He said the last with vehemence. "No more stops." He glared down at Kat once more. "Let's go."

She pushed past him. "Men," she muttered. "Can't live with 'em, can't shoot 'em."

Not waiting for Vince, she slid her skirt up to the tops of her thighs and straddled the Harley. She could drive just as well as he could. If he didn't like it, he could just ride to Port Charlotte with Phil. That brought a smile to her lips. The time together would do them good.

Victory poked a tiny hole in her misery, shored up her confidence. She knew how to play Vince. Whatever had happened, she could win him back.

Vince slung a leg over the seat and scooted in close behind her. It gave her immense pleasure to find that he was still incredibly hard. He'd wanted her, all right. Whatever had stopped him, it wasn't physical.

Just for the hell of it she revved the Harley's engine, long and loud. The next time they had sex, he would be the one doing the pleading, not her. She'd make it so damned *hard* on him, he'd be on his knees begging in no time at all.

She released the clutch and jetted toward the highway in a spray of gravel. The rest of Vince's body went rigid, as well, only this time it had nothing to do with sex and everything to do with fear for his life.

Kat grinned in triumph. *Men.* They just didn't like being controlled by women. Especially the Vincent

Ferrelli types. She arched her spine, jutting her fanny right into the vee of his widespread thighs. The fingers clutching her waist tightened, dug into her flesh, sending a thrill through her.

Oh, yes. She was going to enjoy immensely putting him in his place. Whatever he'd been up to since they parted ways would come out. Kat was sure of it. All she had to do was bide her time and turn up the heat.

IT LOOKED as if the gang was all there when Vince and Kat arrived at the rental house in Port Charlotte. She hopped off the leather seat and smoothed down her skirt. To his extreme irritation, his heart skipped a beat or two as his gaze followed her naturally sensual movements. She was so damned beautiful.

But he wasn't supposed to be dwelling on that particular aspect. He pushed the kickstand into place and swung off the bike. On second thought, he snatched the keys from the ignition just to make sure she didn't take over again.

She shot him a distinctly satisfied look before sauntering up the drive. She twisted her hips as provocatively as possible every step of the way. Vince just shook his head. He'd royally ticked her off by resisting her sexual advances. If she only knew how hard that had been. He exhaled a heavy breath. Oh, well. She'd thank him in the end.

Assuming either one of them survived the mission. Judging by the lethal looks Philip Yu had given him, the two of them weren't going to be buds.

Before following Kat, Vince took a moment to survey the place once more. Two stories, front and rear entrances only. Steel door on front, sliding-glass doors at the patio in back. The entire neighborhood appeared to be rental property, college-age tenants mostly. Parties had still been going on in a couple of the houses when he arrived that morning.

He'd set up observation on the house before dawn. Then he'd followed Kat and Yu when they'd left, though he hadn't known their mission. He had to find out what was in that briefcase as soon as possible. Lucas probably knew by now. The CIA had likely already received word that an unauthorized transfer had gone down. Lucas would send word via Callahan at the first opportunity.

Meanwhile, Vince needed to see what he could ferret out. He shoved the keys into the pocket of his jeans and headed inside. Might as well face the music. The next few minutes would be crucial to the mission as well as his continued good health. He adjusted the weapon concealed at the small of his back. His backup piece was tucked safely into his ankle holster. He was as ready as he was going to get.

He glanced left then right as he made his way to the front door. Callahan would be around here someplace. She'd do what she could to watch his back. But, then, once he got inside he was on his own.

The front door stood ajar since his imminent arrival was expected—if not wanted. As he pushed the door the rest of the way inward he heard Kat's voice.

"He's in or I'm out. No negotiation."

Laced with steel, her words were to the point, her tone about the temperature of a Baptist preacher's brimstone. So, the battle had begun.

"I don't like it."

Another female voice. Vince mentally ran down the list of names Lucas had given him. Leva Vlasov. Twenty-five. A coldhearted rent-to-own type who was best described as a card-carrying member of Psychos-R-Us. Her family had emigrated from Russia when she was only two years old. High-school dropout, former junkie, but a kick-ass inventor. She loved explosives. Had designed a few of her own. If she wasn't stopped, Vince could see her making the *List*. The FBI's Most Wanted list.

"Like I care what you think," Kat retorted arrogantly.

Damn, she was still fearless. He'd been afraid that had changed, but it hadn't. Whether it was the implant or just the years in the Company, she'd bounced all the way back and then some. *Or maybe, it was what you did to her,* a little voice interjected. Helped to make her as ruthless as the very people she sought to bring down.

He gritted his teeth and forced his attention back to the scene playing out only a few yards away in the oversize living room. The blinds were drawn tight, leaving the room only dimly lit by a couple of lamps. Dark paneling and drab furnishings added another layer of shadows to the gloom. The brown leather briefcase was not in sight. A young, white male lounged in one of the overstuffed chairs. Will Adams, twenty-two, loud and obnoxious. A college reject and utter disappointment to his wealthy Massachusetts family. A genius with computers and more at home in the cyberworld than the real one, Will kept the team in petty cash à la his trust fund.

"I think you two bitches should just go outside and settle this the old-fashioned way."

Jamal Johnson, also called J-Man. Weapons expert and top marksman for the team. Kept a perfect four-point-oh in his academics and could dismantle and reassemble any kind of personal weapon made. Suspected in a couple of homicides back home in Chicago, but never charged. Exactly the kind of impressionable youth whose lack of foresight or trust where his own potential was concerned led him to a life of crime. Now he thought he was one of the good guys. Jamal occupied the sofa.

Philip Yu leaned against the mantel of the brick fireplace. He watched the two women squaring off in the center of the room but said nothing. Yu was the oldest of the group at twenty-eight. He was good with computers and highly organized. He had no family, but, from all accounts, had an obsession with the Chinese culture of his forefathers, including the martial arts. He'd never been to college and had spent his youth drifting from the fringes of one Asian gang to another, never really quite *in*. He'd apparently finally found a home with WSA. A place where he thought he could make a difference. Be a good guy, putting his tumultuous early years behind him. Boy, did he have a rude awakening coming to him.

"Why don't you shut up," Leva growled at Jamal.

Vince kicked the door shut behind him. All gazes swung in his direction. Several hands darted to concealed weapons.

"Don't let me interrupt," Vince offered. He took a few steps into the room and gestured to the closest chair. "I'll just have a seat and wait for the verdict." He dropped into the chair and crossed his legs at the ankles. He waved a hand. "Carry on."

"I mean it," Kat reiterated after giving him a cursory glance that spoke volumes about how little her anger at him had abated. Yet, she still stood up for him. "If he goes, I go."

No one said a word. Will looked disinterested. Jamal rolled his eyes and Leva steamed.

Philip Yu pushed off from the fireplace and walked slowly in Vince's direction. This, Vince had expected.

It would be Yu, not Leva, who would present the biggest problem. It had nothing to do with security, however, and everything to do with territorial issues. He wanted Kat for himself. Waiting for hell to freeze over would be a more realistic goal.

Taking his time, his movements deliberate, Yu circled Vince as if trying to decide the best course of action. He paused directly in front of him, arms folded over his chest and asked, "And what would you bring to this group?"

Vince shrugged nonchalantly. "Nothing, maybe." He surveyed the team and cocked his head. "Everything, probably."

"Just kill him and get it over with," Jamal snapped abruptly. He clearly didn't appreciate Vince's attitude.

"This is wack." He shot to his feet and started pacing and making dramatic hand gestures. "We don't need anybody else. The Man won't like it, I can tell you that right now."

The Man. Now Vince was getting someplace.

Still looming over Vince, Yu smirked, enjoying the jabs against him. "I'm afraid we have no openings at the present time, *Mr. Ferrelli.*"

Kat sent a chilling look in Yu's direction.

"However," Yu continued in spite of his obvious inclination to do otherwise, "if a member is willing to risk the consequences of your conditional association, I might be swayed." He apparently was not willing to risk losing Kat entirely. "You see, I have my own rules where association is concerned."

Kat matched Yu's stance. Her feet wide apart, her arms crossed firmly. "I'm willing," she said hotly.

"So be it." Yu looked from Kat to Vince. "I hope you're worth the trouble."

Vince went on instant alert. He was ready and willing to face any challenge Yu put in front of him, but—

Yu snapped his fingers, derailing the rest of the thought. Will, surprisingly quick and agile for a guy so seemingly laid back, jumped to his feet and rushed to a hall closet. He rummaged around about thirty seconds or so while no one else moved or said a word. Vince had a bad feeling. Yu looked entirely too proud of himself for this to be good.

Will returned from his search and plopped a pair of handcuffs in Yu's open palm. Vince sat up a little straighter. Yu held out his free hand and Kat placed her weapon in it, which he promptly passed to Will. Yu then locked one cuff onto Kat's right wrist, led her to the bottom of the stairs then attached the other cuff onto a wrought-iron spindle in the winding staircase railing. Like an obedient child, she sat on the second tread.

Vince surged to his feet. "Whatever you've got in mind should be between the two of us." He glanced at Kat before turning his threatening glare back on Yu. *"Just you and me."*

Yu shook his head slowly from side to side, his smile taunting. "Doesn't work that way. We all had to take a loyalty test. As a member of this team, if Kat vouches for you, she bets her life on your loyalty and your ability. It's the golden rule."

A rush of burning adrenaline sent Vince's heart into a faster rhythm. "We're out then."

Yu only laughed, enjoying the hell out of watching Vince squirm. "Too late. Now listen closely because I will not repeat myself."

Vince stood stock-still, afraid to even breathe for fear of missing one word of Yu's instructions.

"Drive across town to Chamblis Avenue. You'll find a former private residence that serves as a frat house."

Vince started to interrupt when Yu stopped him with an uplifted hand.

Vince clenched his jaw shut, fury boiling up inside him.

"Two weeks ago I crossed paths with a couple of the members of this organization. One of them possesses a certain item that I desire. Get it and bring it to me and she lives." He inclined his head in Kat's direction. "Fail or refuse and she dies."

"You have to let me go with him," Kat demanded, on her feet, and looking far too concerned to pull off the courageous tone in her voice. "He'll need backup."

Yu shook his head. "He goes alone. Interfere and he dies now."

The standoff continued about three seconds. At last, and to Vince's immense relief, Kat dropped back onto the step.

"What the hell kind of item?" Vince demanded. "What do I look for?" Desperation topped out as he weighed how much was at risk versus the information he had been given.

"You'll know it when you see it. The man who currently possesses it is not worthy of its ownership." Yu pulled his 9 mm from his jeans and glanced at his watch. "You have one hour."

Another surge of desperation stabbed Vince. This was insane. "What's the exact address? I need to know where I'm going."

"J-Man will lead the way. He'll also be watching every move you make. Make a mistake and she dies." Yu glanced at his watch again. "Fifty-nine minutes."

Vince sent one last look in Kat's direction. When he would have looked away, her gaze held his. Those green eyes told him the one thing he needed to know: she trusted him.

He wouldn't let her down.

Whether Yu was serious or not, Vince couldn't be

sure. Like the rest of this ragtag team, the guy danced on the edge of psychotic. Pressing the matter to measure just how far Yu would go—if he would really hurt her— considering the way he felt about Kat, was a risk Vince wasn't willing to take.

VINCE HAD STUDIED a map of the Port Charlotte area before leaving D.C. that morning. He knew the approximate location of Chamblis Avenue, but he allowed Jamal to lead the way. He drove a black SUV. The team had access to two SUVs, both black. Expensive rides for university students and their dropout friends. Someone big had to be bankrolling this operation. Someone besides the rich kid with the monthly allowance. The only question was how long would it take the team to earn the right to be *all the way* in. To meet The Man himself.

Maybe they wouldn't. There was always the possibility that they would die following orders without ever really knowing from whom those orders came. Vince was reasonably sure Yu was the key. He was in deeper than the rest. He may have even met with Kovner already.

At the moment Vince didn't give a rat's butt about nailing Kovner. Right now all he had on his mind was keeping Kat safe. If Yu was serious—Vince glanced at his watch—he had just forty-three minutes to retrieve whatever the hell it was Yu wanted and to get it back to him. Another wave of stark fear rushed over Vince. There were few things in this world that scared him, but hurting Kat again, directly or indirectly, definitely did.

J-Man parked in front of a small, neat cottage, but

that wasn't Vince's destination. He'd already recognized the target as easily as if it had been marked with a red bull's-eye. A seventies-style ranch house stuccoed and painted a nasty beige color. The clashing dragons in a fight to the death, trapped forever by an amateur artist's brush above the front door, was like a neon sign screaming This Is The Place!

Someone inside that house had something Yu wanted.

Vince made a U-turn and stashed his Harley a half a block behind J-Man's SUV. Vince took a penlight and a small pry bar from the storage area under his seat and headed in the direction of his target. He nodded at the brooding guy who'd escorted him here as he passed. "I won't be long."

"Yeah, you just go ahead and play the tough guy," Jamal called to Vince's back. "You're dead already. So's that bitch of yours. We don't need her, anyway. We should've ditched her already. Would have if Phil didn't have a thing for her."

Vince stopped and turned back to the cocky SOB tempting his fate without even knowing it. He didn't have time to analyze the crack about the team not needing Kat. "I'll be back," he threatened. "And if you're lucky I'll only break one of your legs for fun."

Jamal made a derisive sound. "Yeah, right. Those Chinese dudes are gonna whip your puny white ass."

Vince ignored the rest of the guy's muttering. He'd wasted enough time already.

Two minutes later he was standing at the front door of the house. It was almost two o'clock in the afternoon and the house echoed a deadly quiet. The tenants were either at school, or work, or sleeping off the previous night's good time. Either way, Vince was going in.

He did the credit-card thing and had the door open in record time, simultaneously palming his weapon. Thankfully no intruder alarms were activated. The damned things were a dime a dozen and everybody seemed to have them nowadays. Not that they presented any real problems, but they were a pain in the rear and wasted valuable time. Then there was the problem that the sound of the alarm usually woke the residents. He didn't need that, either—assuming anyone was home.

The front door led right into the living room, which was lit by a single bare bulb in the unshaded lamp that sat near a shabby sofa. The heavy draperies were closed tight, blocking the afternoon sun. Even in the low light the place looked as if it had been ransacked, but Vince felt reasonably certain that it was nothing more than young-single-male decor.

He took slow, steady breaths in hopes of keeping his heart rate at a reasonable pace. He had to think clearly and move quickly. There was no way to know for sure what he was looking for, but Yu had insisted he would know it when he saw it. Yu desired it greatly. Something personal to him…something from the culture he worshiped, was Vince's best guess.

The living room, kitchen and bathroom yielded nothing. Vince's pulse rate doubled as he moved down the hall toward the bedrooms. He had only thirty-five minutes left. In the first bedroom he found nothing but a sleeping Caucasian male. Bedroom number two rendered much the same, only this sleeping beauty was of Asian descent. Vince's temple started to throb with his mushrooming agitation. He had to hurry. Had to find it…whatever *it* was.

In the third bedroom another man slept, this one also of the Far Eastern persuasion, and with his woman wrapped in his arms. Vince quickly scanned the room as he had the others, using only the small penlight.

Nothing. There was nothing here. What the hell was it that Yu wanted? Vince glanced at the woman and considered whether she could be it. Then he thought of Yu's attachment to Kat and decided against that possibility. Then again, Yu didn't seemed opposed to killing Kat to prove a point.

It wasn't the woman. Vince was sure of it.

He would know it when he saw it, Yu had said.

Then he saw it. A gleaming silver ceremonial sword. Even in the poor illumination produced by the tiny flashlight, the sword was obviously very valuable. That had to be it. No question. The only trouble was it hung on the wall above the bed's headboard. Vince couldn't see any way to retrieve it without waking the slumbering couple. And that would not be a good thing, or a time-wise one. He had to find another way.

Thirty-three minutes.

Sweat rising on his skin, Vince eased to the woman's side of the bed. He shoved the pry bar and weapon into the waistband of his jeans, held the penlight between his teeth and leaned as far over the bed as he dared. Slowly, not even breathing, he reached for the sword.

The image of Kat cuffed to that railing kept zooming through his mind. He had to hurry. Couldn't make a mistake. Couldn't let her down.

His tension eased marginally when he had the sword in his hand. He gritted his teeth, straining against the awkward position until he slowly, quietly, lowered the weapon far enough that he could grasp it with his left hand, as well.

Got it.

Now all he had to do was to get out without waking anyone.

Vince moved slowly, cautiously, across the room…to the door…and into the long, narrow hall. Picking up speed then, the thickly padded carpet muffling the sound of his steps, he made his way back to the living room.

When he reached for the front doorknob the hair on the back of his neck stood on end.

Someone was right behind him.

Vince whipped around, slicing through the air with the sword. The owner leaped back, bowing his body to avoid the sharp edge.

He had a gun. Vince lunged forward and kicked the weapon from his hand. The guy rushed Vince. He tossed the sword aside and went for the guy's midsection.

They tumbled to the floor. The guy managed one blow that landed square on Vince's left cheekbone. He ignored the explosion of pain. The sound of pottery shattering followed the fall of the lamp as they rolled into a table.

Seconds later the other male sleeping beauties came to their friend's aid.

Leaving the first guy temporarily disabled on the floor, Vince took the guy from bedroom number one down easily with a quick pop to his left temple with the dual-purpose pry bar. The other fellow wasn't going to be so easy.

The sword owner staggered to his feet. Vince moved back toward the front door, putting himself between the two men and the sword. He didn't want to use his gun unless it was necessary. Not only did he not want to kill any of these guys, he also didn't want the neighbors alerted to the trouble. He didn't have time to deal with the police.

"You're a dead man," the former sword owner threatened.

Damn. Vince was just about fed up with people saying that.

The second guy made a move.

The wrong one.

He dropped like a rock, his nose bleeding profusely.

The ensuing struggle with the last man standing required some time. Precious time. He was determined. He was good.

But Vince was better.

Vince picked up the sword, leaving the owner unconscious on the floor.

He exited through the front door and quickly checked his watch. Eighteen minutes.

Damn.

He double-timed it back to his Harley.

"I'll take the sword," Jamal demanded as Vince passed him.

"Like hell." Vince didn't slow down. The sword was leverage.

He quickly secured the sword to the bike.

Sixteen minutes.

He sped across town, retracing his route as quickly as he dared.

When he reached the house where Kat was being held, he was off the bike and removing the weapon before Jamal made the turn into the driveway.

With barely one minute to spare, Vince stormed inside, not bothering to knock or to announce himself.

Leva and Will were pacing the living room, both looked startled—and blatantly disappointed—to see him.

Yu stood over Kat, the weapon in his hand aimed directly at her head.

Vince tossed the sword in Yu's direction. "Anything else I can do for you?"

Yu caught the sword by the jewel-embellished handle. He shoved his 9 mm into its usual resting place, never taking his eyes off the prize sword. "Release her," he ordered.

Will obliged, releasing Kat and passing her weapon back to her.

Kat stood, checked the .38, then tucked it away. She absently rubbed at her right wrist where the cuff had no doubt chafed it.

Yu smiled at her. "Looks like your friend is in." He glanced at Vince. "I hope you can keep him in line."

"Don't worry," Kat assured him. "I know how to handle Vince." She flashed Vince a look that he figured he was better off not trying to interpret, then she turned back to Yu. "There's just one thing."

Yu stopped admiring his new toy long enough to focus his full attention in her direction. "And what is that?"

He didn't have time to prepare for the blow, definitely hadn't expected it. Kat sucker punched him in the gut.

"Don't use me in your sick little games again. Next time take my word."

No one uttered a single syllable. They all wore the same startled expression as Yu. When his look of surprise morphed into a grin of amusement as well as respect, everyone relaxed, including Vince.

Yu gifted her with a little bow. "The game point is yours."

"Good." She gave him her back and turned to Vince. "Come with me."

Not about to refute her declaration that she could keep him in line, Vince followed her up the stairs without hesitation. She led the way to the bathroom.

"Sit down," she ordered.

It wasn't until he passed the mirror hanging over the sink that Vince realized the extent of the beating he'd taken. His cheek was a little swollen and his lip was busted. All in all, though, he looked pretty damned good considering the odds had been three to one.

As ordered, he took a seat on the closed toilet lid.

He could relax, at least for the moment. He was in. This mission might just be salvageable, after all.

Kat dampened a washcloth with cold water and pressed it against his cheek. The cold felt great, but her nearness felt even better. She knelt between his knees and dabbed at his bleeding lip.

"You could have been killed," she scolded softly.

She was right. He didn't bother arguing.

Vince watched her intent expression, his body reacting to both her proximity and the obvious affection he saw in her eyes. For the hundredth time he wondered how he'd let her get away. And, considering their past, what had made her use him for her Romeo profile? It made no sense at all. Did she still feel something for him—besides anger and bitterness? Or was it simply some sort of payback that he didn't yet understand?

Cool fingers traced his lower lip, made him tremble inside. She was looking at his mouth now—not with concern but with longing.

How could he let this thing between them happen without some answers? When this was over, and she had her memory back, she'd hate him even more than she already did.

She eased closer, her mouth only inches from his.

He could feel her pull…could feel the temptation of that lush mouth…

But he couldn't let this happen.

He pulled back, took the cloth from her hand and quickly stood when she sat back on her heels to look up at him in surprise…annoyance…something on that order. He didn't miss the flicker of hurt on her face as he sidled away from her. Dammit, he was going to hurt her either way.

Feigning interest in the condition of his face, he peered into the mirror over the sink. "Those guys did a hell of a job on me," he commented offhandedly. "I think this—"

The definitive click of a weapon engaging shut him up.

Kat nudged the tip of the .38's barrel against his temple. "Okay, big guy," she said, her tone every bit as lethal as the weapon now aimed at his head. "Just who the hell are you?"

Chapter Four

Vince stood absolutely still and considered his limited options.

The .38 now boring a hole in his right temple was loaded. He'd watched Kat check it just minutes ago. Not to mention that there were four more people downstairs who would like nothing better than to blow his head off simply for the sport of it.

He'd just have to wing it.

He focused on Kat's reflection in the mirror. Her respiration was controlled. That was good. Her expression calm. Also good. But her finger was snugged just a little too tightly around that trigger for comfort.

That was *not* good.

"What gives, Kitty Kat?" he asked softly, the huskiness in his voice a very real, undeniable result of being alone with her for more than ten seconds, present circumstances not withstanding. "You tired of me already?"

The muzzle pressed even more firmly into his skull.

"Who the hell are you and what did you do with the real Vince Ferrelli?"

He didn't dare move a muscle. In fact, holding his breath seemed like the smart thing to do about now. Her gaze never deviated from her target, not even a fleeting glance in the mirror so that he might read her intent in those big green eyes. He had to assume the worst—that her real memory was somehow scrambled with the implanted one—but hope for the best. He'd been an optimist his whole life, why change now?

"I left him behind. He's dead."

Vince didn't miss the little catch in her breathing when he said the "dead" word. A muscle contracted in his jaw. If this didn't work—if she was seriously damaged—he was screwed. And Lucas and Casey were going to be extremely disappointed that he hadn't made it past the first twenty-four hours.

"What the hell is that supposed to mean?" she demanded tautly, a little something besides anger in her voice. A hint of vulnerability, maybe?

Vince stared at her in the mirror, willing her to look at him with every ounce of determination he possessed, while he told her the truth that had burned in the back of his brain for four endless years. "Because he took you for granted. He didn't understand that he was screwing up the best thing he'd ever had." Hesitation slowed him. He'd just been brutally honest and the Kat he'd once known might never know it. "That man no longer exists," he tacked on for good measure. "I guess you're stuck with me now."

An acute silence ruled for what couldn't have been more than a few seconds, but felt like hours.

She lowered her weapon as abruptly as she had taken aim. "It's a damn good thing." She set the safety and plunked it onto the vanity's faux marble surface. "I was just about sick of your disappearing acts."

Vince exhaled the breath he'd been holding. Talk about bad hair days. He didn't want to think what kind of mess he'd have at the moment if his hunch had been wrong. Of course the .38 would have damaged a lot more than his hair. He faced her, slid his arms around her waist and pulled her against him.

"It won't happen again." He nuzzled between those fiery red curls and pressed a kiss to her forehead. "Nothing will take me away from you again." He wished that was true, but he knew even if he got her through this mission, she would reject him the moment she had her real memory back.

Her palms slid upward from his waist to his shoulders, singeing a path along his back. She touched his damaged lip with one soft fingertip. "Let me make that better before I have to go." She kissed his battered mouth.

He closed his eyes and tried his level best not to let this get out of hand. The blood was rushing toward the part of his anatomy that needed it the least at the moment. "Where are you going?" His words were scarcely a whisper as she kissed her way along his bruised cheek. Slow, lingering kisses that were as light as a butterfly's wings but as erotic as anything he'd ever experienced. His arms tightened around her, pressing her body more firmly against his. She felt so damned good.

Without warning she pulled back, smiling widely, clearly pleased with herself. "I have a class." She rubbed his armed-and-ready crotch. "Save it for later."

Slack-jawed, Vince could only stare at her retreating back.

"AND WHAT DID THAT accomplish?"

The professor's commanding voice echoed in the large half-empty lecture hall. Kat listened, not really hearing, as he elaborated on the aftereffects, social, economic and so forth, related to the fall of the Berlin Wall. European history wasn't exactly boring, but she had other things on her mind today.

Such as Vince's startling confession.

She shifted in her seat and thought about what he'd said. He wasn't going to take her for granted anymore. He promised not to disappear on her again. The intensity of the emotions his words stirred inside her scared her to death. She swallowed a little lump of emotion.

Did this mean he loved her?

A frown furrowed her brow. How was she supposed to feel about that? She loved Vince. She knew that... didn't doubt it for a second.

But how did love fit into who she was right now? Certainly a house in suburbia and a baby carriage had no place in her life now or any time soon as far as she could see. Her chest tightened. But something about him made her long for those everyday things…made her ache to make what they had last forever.

Ridiculous.

Kat rolled her eyes at her own stupidity. She was a WSA agent, for heaven's sake. Her life was too danger-ous, too uncertain to even consider permanence of any sort. For that matter, so was Vince's.

For long minutes she considered how she came to be at this place. Her mind told her immediately that she'd met Philip Yu here, on campus, and as their friendship progressed he had invited her to join his cause. But that didn't feel precisely right. Every move she made, such as today at the train station, felt second nature. Sure she'd done a little undercover work for her uncle who owned a P.I. agency down in Richmond, but somehow that didn't feel like an accurate explanation. It had to be, though. Philip had checked her references.

Yet how could she feel so uncomfortable in her own skin? She propped her elbow on the table in front of her and massaged her forehead. The dull ache never quite seemed to go away. At times it was easier to ignore than others, but it never really left her. Headaches this per-sistent couldn't be chalked up to simple sinus compli-cations. As far as she could tell she didn't have the first allergy. Besides, the pain was localized.

Maybe she should get it checked out at the univer-sity infirmary. It couldn't hurt, she supposed.

She glanced back at the door and wondered what Vince was doing. He'd refused to stay at the house. Considering Leva and Jamal were hanging out there, she couldn't blame him. He would wait for her, he'd insisted. He'd certainly never done that before. Maybe he had turned over a new leaf.

That remained to be seen.

The abrupt shuffle of papers and books startled Kat back to the here and now. Class was over. Everyone else was already up and heading for the door. Kat hastily shoved her book into her bag and grabbed her purse.

"Miss Moore."

Kat glanced at the podium where Professor Damrus still stood, studying her.

"Yes." She gathered her things and moved to the main aisle between the long rows of tables and chairs. "I'm sorry, Professor, did you have a question?"

He waited until she was halfway to the podium before responding. "You seemed a little distracted today, Miss Moore."

Kat swore silently. If he only knew. "Yes, sir." She slung her bag over one shoulder and manufactured a smile. "I guess I was. I won't let it happen again."

Professor Damrus stood about medium height, was thin and relatively handsome for a man of forty. He had classic taste in clothes; the navy-blue pin-striped suit was conservative, expensive. Small gold wire-rimmed glasses, the round sort, perched on his thin blade of a nose. His dark hair was heavily peppered with gray, but his dark brown eyes were his most prominent feature. They were clear and intelligent, and entirely too perceptive.

"Trouble with the opposite sex?" he suggested. One dark eyebrow arched above the glasses.

Trouble with sex period, she almost said, but didn't. She averted her gaze, a little reluctant to discuss the matter with him. "Nothing I can't handle," she said pointedly. Where did this guy get off asking her about her sex life?

"Wait a moment and I'll walk out with you." He moved to his desk and placed papers to be graded and a couple of books in his soft-sided leather briefcase. He looked up long enough to offer her a smile. "This is my final class of the day."

She dredged up a patient smile. "Mine, too."

His gaze lingered on her for a couple of beats too long before returning to his task. For the first time since Professor Damrus took over the class, Kat felt a twinge of apprehension in his presence. It was something about the way he had looked at her. Or maybe it was the lapse into expectant silence that sent off warning bells.

More likely it was her inflated paranoia of late. She spent half of her time questioning herself, the other half questioning the motivation of everyone else. Common sense told her the university was lucky to have found someone so well qualified in the middle of a session. Professor Pratt had taken emergency medical leave, giving the school no notice.

Enter Professor Damrus— Who was currently freaking Kat out with his creepy behavior. She was suddenly very glad that Vince was waiting for her just outside. *Okay, girl, you're overreacting.*

The professor moved up beside Kat. "Shall we?" He gestured to the rear exit.

She nodded, relieved he was finally ready to go. "Sure."

Her heart rate went from seventy to one hundred in the space of three beats. Her skin felt clammy. The door suddenly looked a very long way away.

"I've looked at your file, Miss Moore. You're a very diligent student."

Kat tamped down her surprise. He was new, maybe he'd reviewed the files of all of his students. Then again, when one considered the size of the university and the number of classes he conducted, that idea appeared a bit of a stretch.

"Thank you," she said hesitantly.

He paused at the door. Kat had the overwhelming urge to run like hell. She scolded herself. This was ridiculous. Was she having paranoid delusions as well as headaches? Maybe she did need to go to the infirmary.

Professor Damrus studied her a moment. "Don't let anything or anyone distract you from your goal, Miss Moore. It would be a mistake."

Those dark brown eyes looked so fiercely determined that Kat could only stare for a moment. "I appreciate your concern," she finally said. "I'll be fine."

He nodded. "Good. I'm here if you need someone to talk to." As he walked away, he called over his shoulder, "See you on Thursday."

Kat stared after the professor until he turned a corner and disappeared. To say the conversation had unnerved her would be a vast understatement. She felt certain the exchange was free of sexual undercurrent. It wasn't about sex. It was…he was warning her… Her grade point average was outstanding. She had perfect attendance. So she'd been a little distracted today. It wasn't the end of the world. Why would he feel the need to do that?

She sighed. Maybe she was making too much of it.

Maybe Professor Damrus simply wanted his students to pay attention in class. Or maybe, since he was so new, he just wanted to connect and he used the topic as a means to an end.

Shaking her head, Kat went off in search of Vince. She had plans for him. Plans that involved lots and lots of physical torture. Like this afternoon when she'd left him as hard as a rock and ready to do anything she told him.

Oh, yes. He would pay for making her wait. And they were nowhere near even.

Kat abruptly halted in her tracks.

Massive Greek-revival-style columns lined the portico that wrapped all the way around the history building. Leaning against one of those columns was Vince. Standing not two feet in front of him was a blonde wearing tight jeans and a bare-the-belly-button midriff top. It might have been the grin on Vince's face, then again it could have been the blonde's rich laughter. Either one or both sent fury roaring through Kat like an out-of-control freight train. A fine red mist swam in front of her eyes.

Kat started forward again, moving faster with every step she took. Maybe this was why he'd been so ready to admit his shortcomings. Her temper rocketed so completely beyond control that she wasn't sure she could speak rationally.

Vince glanced up. Their gazes collided. His relaxed posture stiffened.

"Well, well," Kat remarked as she struck a clearly indignant pose along side the blonde. "Isn't this cozy?"

"Oh, hey. You must be Kat." The blonde smiled at Kat and thrust out her hand. "The name's Blue. Your friend here hasn't shut up about you since I tried to hit on him."

Some of the steam went out of Kat's outrage. She shook the woman's hand grudgingly, briefly. "Really?"

Blue nodded vigorously. Kat could see why she was called Blue. The woman had the bluest eyes Kat had ever seen. It didn't help that she was gorgeous, too.

"Well, Vince, maybe I'll see you around." Blue beamed a smile in his direction, then turned to Kat and winked. "He's a keeper."

As Blue disappeared into the crowd of students loitering around, Kat folded her arms over her chest and glared at Vince. "Is this why you insisted on coming with me? So you could peruse the babes?"

Vince grinned. "I like it when you get jealous."

Kat was the one to stiffen this time. "I am not jealous," she hissed. The very idea. If she were the jealous type she'd never have survived their long separations. An ache arced through her at the thought of being separated from Vince. If he left again, she wasn't sure she could take it.

"Look." Vince grabbed her sleeve and tugged her closer. "The lady flirted with me a little," he admitted. "And I told her all about you. Any law against that?"

Well, the woman had known her name. He could be telling the truth. God, she hated this feeling of insecurity.

She tiptoed and deposited a kiss on Vince's bruised cheek. "I guess not." She felt a smile kicking up one corner of her mouth. "Considering your battle scars she probably thought you were some kind of bad boy."

Vince pulled Kat into his arms and looked deeply into her eyes. "The only time I'm bad is when I'm with you."

Kat's smile was genuine this time. Those jade-colored eyes shimmered with affection. Vince would walk across hot coals anytime to see that smile. God, he'd missed her smile. Missed her. The last of the tension seeped from his muscles. He and Blue had cut their meeting a little too close. As a cover she had taken an application and had asked several people how they liked the professors and the class offerings. Vince had watched her work the crowd. She was good. There was no reason for anyone to be suspicious.

Lucas had sent word to Vince via Blue that the intelligence lost in the briefcase in D.C. had been recovered from backup files. Steps were being taken to defuse the impact its falling into wrong hands would have. Vince didn't need to be concerned with recovering it.

Now that Vince was in and Kat's condition had been verified, he was to see the original mission through in the hope of bringing down the man behind the World Security Agency.

All he had to do was keep Kat happy and Yu off his back.

A piece of cake.

"How about we get out of here?" Vince offered in a tone that suggested a lot more than just a ride on his Harley.

She tilted her head back and gazed up at him in challenge. "Only if I can drive."

Vince reached into his pocket and retrieved the key. He dangled it in front of her. "*Only* if you promise to be good."

She snatched the key from his hand and backed out of his arms. "I'm always good."

Minutes later they were cruising up Highway 1. It felt good to be on the open road. Vince held on tightly to the woman who fit so perfectly in the curve of his body. He put the past as well as the future out of his mind and focused on the present. On being with Kat. Neither of them had the promise of tomorrow, they might as well enjoy today.

Before going to school, she had traded the uptight gray suit for black, curve-hugging jeans and a black tank top that showed just enough cleavage to whet his appetite. She looked amazing.

Kat slowed, taking an exit that was new to Vince. She drove through a small, populated area, then turned onto a long, deserted stretch of road.

"Where are we going?" he asked loud enough that she could hear over the roar of the Harley's engine.

She grinned. "You'll see."

Dusk was settling when they reached the end of the road and parked the bike. Woods rolled for miles on either side, but the attraction was right in front of them. The Potomac River cut through the landscape, its dark water lapping softly against the shore. Music borne of solitude and nature drifted on the air. A bird's call…the ever-moving water…the whisper of the wind in the trees.

Kat took his hand in hers and tugged him toward a narrow path that meandered between the water and the woods. Vince laced his fingers with hers and followed, wondering what it was that had drawn her here. The water? Or the solitude?

As they sat, waiting and watching, a full moon rose, then hung almost low enough to touch the treetops. It was so peaceful a person could almost forget the rest of the world. Vince decided that was why they were here. Kat had wanted or needed the time alone. They hadn't spoken. The silence felt comfortable, though.

At least until she asked her first question.

"How long have we known each other, Vince?" She paused to stare out over the water. Moonlight glinted against its dark depths adding an element of danger to its allure.

He hoped like hell this wasn't a trick question. Was the truth the same answer that was coded in the implant? There was only one way to find out.

"Four years and three months." It was the truth.

She thought about that for a while, then fired off her next question. "Did you know my uncle Max?"

Uncle Max was the code name for her cover. Yu and the others believed Kat had learned her extracurricular activities working for an uncle who operated a shady private investigations business down in Richmond. He'd been a demolitions man in the military and passed on the knowledge of his beloved hobby to his favorite niece.

"Sure, I know Max. He's a real character."

She stopped and looked at Vince. Even in the

ghostly moonlight he could see the confusion on her face. The questions in her eyes. "Why doesn't he feel real to me?" She looked out over the water again. "*I* don't feel real to me."

His gut clenched at the idea of what she must be going through. She was a highly trained operative. No doubt her mind was working overtime to regain control from the implant. He ached to tell her the truth, but he couldn't take the risk. He'd been warned that a step like that could confuse her, could disrupt the tenuous balance of the implant.

The only thing he could do was be there for her. Vince took her face in his hands. Gently he turned her gaze toward his. "You're real, all right." He brushed his lips against hers, the sting reminding him of his recent injury. He ignored it. "Very real," he murmured.

He kissed her tenderly at first, allowing the moment to last. Then he deepened the kiss, relearning the sweetness of her mouth, the wickedness of her tongue. She arched her slender body against his and he wondered if he would have the strength to pull away.

Heat flared in his body, quick little bursts of sensation that disrupted his equilibrium. The feel of her breasts pressed against his chest was very nearly more than he could bear.

He pulled back, peered down into those lust-glazed eyes. "Any more questions?"

She leaned her forehead against his chin. "I know it sounds crazy," she said breathlessly. She tilted her head back and looked at him once more, her arms still draped around his shoulders. "It's like I know who I am, what I've done in my life." She shrugged halfheartedly. "I know about us. But somehow it's like a book I've read instead of things I've actually experienced."

Vince stilled, a chill chasing away the heat she'd kindled inside him. "Maybe it's just stress." He pushed those silky curls back from her face. "You know, the pressure of keeping Yu happy and going to school." He inclined his head toward one shoulder in a gesture of doubt. "All you've been through with me maybe. You know, just stress."

He felt her body tense in his arms. "Could be."

"All I'm saying is that it's probably nothing," he amended quickly. Obviously he shouldn't have brought up the part about the trouble she'd had with him. *Smooth move, Ferrelli.*

She sighed again. "Phil can be a jerk. Sometimes I don't even know why I let myself get involved with him."

"He had to be sure about me," Vince interjected, hoping to put the brakes on that line of analysis.

"Yeah, well. He ticked me off." Kat pulled out of Vince's arms and started to walk back toward the clearing where they'd left his bike. "He's on this power trip. I'm not sure I trust his motives anymore."

Vince kept quiet and let her talk.

"The others didn't want me onboard in the first place. But Phil ignored their protests." She looked at Vince for a moment before continuing. "I think you should keep an eye on him. I'm not sure we can trust him where you're concerned."

Jealousy reared its ugly head. "I think he has a thing for you." He made the statement as nonchalantly as he could, but still it came out sounding possessive.

She sent another one of those lingering sidelong glances in Vince's direction. "You did stay gone an awful long time this time," she said frankly. "I was lonesome."

His fingers curled into fists. "Does that mean the two of you had something going on?"

She shrugged. "Not on the level you think."

Vince was going to kill him.

"Why don't you tell me exactly what level the two of you reached?"

It was more of a command than a question. One uttered savagely. Vince barely recognized his own voice.

Her hands found a home on her hips and she rolled her eyes. "Get over it, Vince. It was nothing physical. It was just an attraction. That's all. We didn't act on it. I was always telling him about the great Vince Ferrelli. Maybe that's why he doesn't like you."

Her assurances in no way assuaged Vince's agitation. It mushroomed, growing and growing into a major storm.

"That's good to know," he said tightly.

Kat flung her arms in frustration. "I cannot believe you're jealous." She huffed disdainfully. "You stayed gone all that time while I—mind you—had no idea where you were and what you were doing, and now you're feeling possessive. Listen up, Ferrelli, if I'd slept with Phil, I can't see where you would have any right to complain."

She stopped, planted her fists on her hips once more and glowered at him. "Admit it. I'm right and you know it."

He grabbed her by the shoulders and gave her a little shake. "Don't play this game with me, Kat. If the man touches you—" it took a moment for him to compose himself "—if he so much as looks at you the wrong way, I'll kill him." He knew exactly how irrational his tirade sounded, but at that moment he meant every word of it. For the first time in his life he wanted to break a guy's neck over a woman. *"You belong to me,"* he added hoarsely.

He'd lost it.

Shaking with the intensity of his emotions, he released her and plowed his fingers through his hair. He ordered himself to back off and to pull it together. Kat was glaring at him, those green eyes glittering with outrage.

"I don't *belong* to anyone," she said, her tone furious. "If you want the right to call me yours, you have to earn it. And so far, buster, you're way behind the curve."

Vince exhaled in defeat as she stomped away. Maybe there was more of the real Kat in that implant than anyone knew. One thing was certain, he had his work cut out for him in more ways than one. He had to get his head screwed on straight and to stop letting the past and the regret he harbored color his perspective.

Piece of cake, all right.

Too bad he was a pie man.

Chapter Five

Disgusted with herself, Kat wanted to die.

"Oh, God," she muttered beneath her breath. How could she admit to Vince how screwed up she was? She ran her fingers through her hair and twisted it into a loose knot on top of her head, then secured it with a couple of pins. To her supreme irritation, corkscrew wisps immediately slipped loose, draping down around her face and neck. She hated having curly hair.

Frustrated with far too many aspects of herself, she closed her eyes and basked in the memory of Vince's fingers in her hair. The way he'd held her face in his hands while he kissed her so thoroughly. She shivered as heat raced through her even now. Thinking about that kiss would not be prudent in her current vulnerable state.

Speaking of vulnerable, she glanced over her shoulder at the man still sleeping soundly in her bed. Yearning surged inside her. How she wanted to crawl back into that bed, wake him, and make long, slow love.

The dark hair and skin he'd inherited from his Italian ancestors contrasted starkly against the white pillowcase. She loved the bold angles and lines of his face. His brow was straight and just a touch heavy, his nose strong, almost aquiline. A night's beard growth covered that chiseled jaw, making him look dangerous and incredibly sexy. The bruise above his cheekbone and the split in those masterfully carved lips added the perfect dash of vulnerability to his tough-guy exterior. Her heart pounded out a little tattoo, keeping rhythm with the desire singing through her veins.

Her visual exploration continued along muscled arms resting on his pillow on either side of his head, then downward to a sculpted torso that made her breath stall in her lungs. She followed a line of silken hair that narrowed and plunged out of sight beneath the white sheet shielding that awesome body from the hips down. Her mouth parched at the memory of other assets barely concealed by the clinging cotton fabric.

On a physical level she'd wanted desperately to make love with him last night after they'd returned to the house. Her intimate position—between his thighs on the Harley—was very nearly her undoing. But her anger had kept an emotional distance between them. Once sleep had claimed them, however, their bodies had taken over. Kat had awakened in what could only be called a compromising position. Fortunately for her, she'd been able to wiggle from his captive hold and escape without waking him.

She wondered if he was always such a sound sleeper.

A frown pinched her expression. She should know that about him, shouldn't she?

Her mind was a total blank on the subject of his sleeping habits, like so many other areas lately. There had to be something wrong with her. A brain tumor or something.

Kat exhaled a disgusted breath and pushed the troubling thought away. Phil would be waiting for her. She'd come back for Vince after this morning's briefing. She could fill him in. Right now she was in far too vulnerable a place to touch him or to even talk to him.

As she stowed her 9 mm—the weapon she usually carried—into the waistband of her jeans, she crossed the room, then hesitated at the door to take a last look at the man who ruled her every thought, hope and dream. A kind of sadness welled inside her. There was something wrong with this whole scenario. She just didn't know what it was.

Maybe she was better off not knowing.

"Where's your partner?" Phil demanded the moment she descended the last tread of the staircase. He stared haughtily at her from his position of authority in the ragged recliner that served as the makeshift focal point in the living room.

She looked straight into those insolent eyes and gave him tit for tat. "Resting." She took her seat on the couch with Jamal and Will. "Trust me, he needs it after last night."

Laughter tittered between the two sprawled lazily next to her on the couch.

Renewed fury swept across Phil's tense features. "If he can't be ready to perform on a moment's notice, then we don't need him." He shoved a fresh clip into his weapon for emphasis.

She'd had enough of this crap yesterday. It was time to move on. Kat leaned forward and braced her elbows on her knees. "Oh, he can perform, honey. Any place, anytime. You can trust me on that one, too."

Her innuendo antagonized him she knew, but she couldn't resist. She'd grown tired of his power trip…of that annoying flexing of his possessive muscle. He was the leader, but they were all supposed to be equal.

"That was a good one, Kat woman," Jamal chuckled. "You might be good for something, after all."

"Shut up," Leva snarled, ignoring the seething look Kat tossed her way. "You're all worthless."

"Let's see you breach the Pentagon's cyber security," Will shot back. "The only thing you know how to do is blow stuff up." He thrust his arms upward in an exaggerated gesture. "Boom!"

If looks could kill… Considering the poisonous glare focused on Will right now, Kat was certain the kid would drop dead any minute.

Phil stood, dragging all gazes to him. "Enough." He aimed a chilling look at Kat. "See this disruption your new friend has caused already. You assured me that you could keep him in line. You keep talking about trust, did I make a mistake trusting you on that score?"

Kat held up a hand. "All right. All right. I'll keep my remarks to myself from now on."

The roundabout apology did nothing to placate his

fury. "This briefing cannot begin without the presence of the entire team. If your friend—"

"Are we doing this or not?" Leva demanded. "We've had nothing but trouble since you let her in." She shifted an accusatory glower in Kat's direction. "I told you we didn't need her in the first place."

Kat smiled and relaxed into the lumpy cushions of the tattered couch. "You think your quirky design ability is all it takes to get the job done? It takes more than a twisted vision to strategically place a device. Not to mention the skill needed to get in and out without getting caught." Kat tapped her right temple. "If memory serves me, that's where you fall down."

Leva's face turned a violent shade of red. "I'm going to get you. Wait and see."

Kat's smile widened. "Promises, promises."

"Get Ferrelli down here, *now,*" Phil ordered, his murderous expression announcing more clearly that he'd reached the end of his rope than his savage tone.

THE SECOND Kat had left their room, Vince had sprung from the bed and thrown on his clothes. He'd pretended to be sleeping so she would go join the others without him. It was their first night together after his extended absence; as far as the rest of the gang knew, she had worn him out. At least he hoped that's what they would assume. He knew the ploy wouldn't buy him much time, but every minute counted. He needed to check out the other bedrooms, Yu's in particular.

The sooner Vince made a direct connection to the mastermind behind WSA, the sooner he'd be able to get Kat out of danger. That also meant ending their time together. He couldn't dwell on the downside right now, her safety and the mission—in that order—had to be top priority.

Jamal's room, the first room he entered, didn't offer much in the way of helpful intelligence. The kid had a stockpile of weapons that would make a hard-core survivalist salivate. Weapons cleaning materials, manuals and not much else. One door down, Leva's room offered nothing, which meant she had a "shop" somewhere on the premises or nearby. All boomers liked their playhouses.

In sharp contrast, poor-little-rich-kid Will had three laptops, two desktop computers, and an assortment of other hardware in his room. The place looked as if he'd recently robbed a local Gateway store. Not an instrument of destruction in sight. Then again, Vince supposed that depended upon what the kid was doing with his electronic toys.

Moving on, near the top of the stairs Vince listened to make sure the whole group was still assembled downstairs in the living room. Leva and Kat argued vehemently. Vince lifted a skeptical eyebrow. He had a bad feeling those two were going to come to blows before too long. Maybe Leva wanted Yu all to herself. That worked for Vince. They could live happily ever after in federal prison.

Satisfied that the group was preoccupied, Vince moved a little further down the hall. Yu's room was, of course, the last one. The cherished ceremonial sword Vince had appropriated for him held a place of honor on the wall above his bed.

Slowly, trying not to make a sound, Vince opened drawer after drawer. He carefully sifted through the items, making sure he left each drawer just as he'd found it.

Nothing.

He moved to the closet, picked through the clothes quickly since there were few, then checked the top shelf and the two shoe boxes on the floor.

Nada.

Vince straightened and scanned the room once more. The briefcase Kat had lifted from the CIA agent had disappeared quickly enough. He'd checked under the bed already. Yu had probably turned it over to his contact before leaving D.C. Then again, Callahan would have spotted any move by Yu since she had no doubt been tagging along somewhere behind them.

As Vince turned to leave, something in his peripheral vision snagged his attention. He turned back to the unmade bed. Peeking from beneath the pillowcase was a slip of paper. Vince started in that direction. How had he missed that before?

The sound of footfalls on the stairs jerked his gaze toward the door. He froze. He quickly measured the distance to the door then judged it against the possibility of diving for what could be evidence.

"Vince!"

Kat.

He swore.

Then he made a decision and went for the evidence.

He shoved the paper into his pocket and slipped into the hall. Kat was already in the room they'd shared last night. Vince moved silently toward the closest door, the one on his left. He eased into the bathroom a split second before she came back out into the hall looking for him.

Pulling the door open wide as if he was just exiting, he adopted a broad smile. "Morning," he said huskily. He plowed his fingers through his hair then stretched as if he could still use another forty winks.

The annoyance tightening her features eased. "You're not getting off to a good start," she chastised. "I wouldn't push my luck if I were you. They're waiting for us." She pivoted and started toward the stairs.

Vince caught her easily, tugging her around to face him. "Is that any way to say good morning?" He touched her cheek, allowed his fingertips to trail along the line of her jaw, then he kissed the tip of her pert little nose. He felt her shiver. "I didn't like waking up without you."

He thought about the way she had looked at him this morning. Though he hadn't seen her, he'd felt her eyes on him. Had heard the subtle change in her breathing. She liked what she saw. He definitely liked what he saw.

What a pair they were.

She didn't remember the past and he couldn't forget it.

She glared up at him, any signs of lust or approval long gone. "You'd better get on the ball, Vince. You're making me look bad."

He acknowledged her reprimand with a humble nod. "You're right. I promise I'll behave from now on." He tapped the spot he'd just kissed. "But I have to tell you I barely got any sleep at all last night. I couldn't stop looking at you long enough to doze off."

She rolled her eyes and pulled free of his hold. "Just don't make a habit of it." She turned away quickly, but not quickly enough for him to miss the rapidly fluttering pulse at the base of her throat.

A satisfied smile slid across his face. No matter how tough she tried to play it, she was just as hung up on him as he was on her—at least as long as she was under the implant's influence anyway.

As he followed her down the stairs he thought about the way he'd danced on the edge last night. He'd told her that she belonged to him. He had to keep thoughts like that out of his head or he'd end up with more emotional baggage than he could carry. He was damn close to that now.

Damn close.

Yu was not a happy camper when the two of them joined the rest of the group. A vein throbbed in his forehead. Judging by the set of his jaw, Vince figured he'd cracked the enamel of his teeth by now. The guy was seriously ticked. Though he shouldn't, Vince enjoyed it immensely.

"If you're going to be part of this team, Ferrelli," Yu began, his voice as tight as the muscles straining in his face, "you will cooperate fully with my orders."

Vince pulled up the side chair he'd used the day before and settled into it. "I wasn't sure I was invited to your private meetings just yet," he said offhandedly. "You're sure there's not some other test you'd like me to take?"

"If you're in," Yu told him, his dark gaze shooting daggers, "you're in. And once you're in, the only way out is feetfirst."

Vince met that lethal gaze with a murderous one of his own. "I think I've got the picture now."

"We've wasted enough time." Yu turned to the others assembled and waiting for his instructions. "Are you ready to field test your new device?" This question he directed to Leva.

She smiled—something too evil to be completely human. "Been ready."

Yu nodded. "J-Man, you take Leva and Will." He glanced at Vince. "Kat and Ferrelli will ride with me."

Vince's antennae had gone up at the mention of "field test." Since he knew Leva's specialty to be demolitions, he had to assume that they were about to test her latest design. If they were field testing already, they would soon be prepping for a mission. Dread pooled in his gut. He didn't really care how dangerous the mission turned out to be, as long as he could keep Kat safe.

KAT GLANCED BACK at Vince as Phil parked the SUV next to the one Jamal had driven. Vince looked preoccupied. Phil just looked pissed off.

The trip to the remote testing site had been silent and fraught with tension. She shot a look at their driver. These guys needed serious one-on-one time. To just go on and duke it out—get it over with. Kat considered suggesting it, but wasn't sure if she could trust Phil to fight fairly. Funny thing was, she'd trusted him completely until a few days ago.

But there was something different now. He'd thrown up a wall around himself, as if he was guarding some secret the rest of them couldn't know. She wouldn't have been so suspicious if it had started with Vince's arrival, but that wasn't the case. She'd noted the change in Phil days ago.

He was the only one who had the privilege of talking with the man in charge. That hadn't really bothered Kat, either, until now. It didn't feel right…but she couldn't put her finger on specifically what part was wrong. Like everything else, her thinking was skewed in that area, as well.

Kat climbed out of the vehicle and started toward Leva and the others.

A couple of rustic tables sat out in the open. Three gleaming metal cases lay side by side on one table. The tools of Leva's trade. Beyond the tables, on the far side of the clearing, were a couple of rundown buildings. Phil had found this place two weeks ago. Judging by the narrow access road and the surrounding undergrowth, no one ever came out here. Walled in by dense woods on all sides, they didn't have to worry about being seen. Phil had even gone to the trouble of setting up perimeter alarms. If anyone got within two hundred yards of the place, they would all know it. The unlucky visitor would know it, too. Only he wouldn't live to tell about it.

Jamal glanced at Kat and burst out laughing.

"Something funny, J-Man?" Though she laced her voice with anger, she'd learned that when dealing with these guys to keep her focus. Let them see what she wanted them to, and always, always, keep a level head. That way they couldn't catch her off guard. She didn't know how she knew that technique, maybe her uncle had taught her, but it worked.

"Oh, nah, man," he assured her, still obviously amused. "I was just thinking 'bout something Leva here said."

Kat gifted Leva with a withering look. The witch just didn't know when to quit. She kept pushing and pushing. One of these days she was going to get what she was asking for. In a big way.

"We'll run through the drill a couple of times first," Yu told them. "Since we won't need these fine facilities after today, we'll see if Leva has managed to work her magic for us."

Leva patted one of the silver cases. "It's my best work yet," she boasted with a cocky tilt of her head.

Will placed a laptop on the other table and booted it up. As the software logo spread across the screen, he explained, "I used the target building's schematics to create a simulation." He looked from Kat to Leva. "A kind of game with you two as the players. I'll run the sim for you. If you disagree with my suggested egress route, we can alter it."

Kat watched as the blueprint of the target building loaded onto the screen. "Very cool, Will," she commented. The guy was a genius. *Too bad he was wasting his life with this bunch of losers.*

Kat tensed.

She was here. What did that make her? She blinked. Where the hell had that thought come from? They were the good guys. Risked their lives on every mission to make the world a safer place. She struggled to slow her respiration. Stay calm. It was just a mistake. She'd meant that Will should have stayed in school…should have developed his potential to a higher level. Her tension eased marginally.

"Before we get to the sim," Leva said, calling attention back to her, "I have something for our newest member." She winked at Jamal.

Kat immediately went on alert. Anything Leva had up her sleeve would be bad news.

Before Kat could demand to know what she was talking about, Leva removed a plain brown paper package from one of her cases and tossed it to Vince. He caught it in both hands.

"You said you expected another test," she challenged. "Open it. I made it just for you." She winked conspiratorially. "Just to make things interesting."

Kat lunged toward Vince. "Don't open it."

Jamal held her back. "Don't be no spoilsport, Kat woman. Let the man have his fun."

"Back off, J-Man," she growled, then turned back to Vince. "Don't open it." Her heart shuddered in her chest then kicked into high gear, pumping pure fear.

Vince's gray gaze collided with hers. If he was worried, it didn't show. But, dammit, he needed to be worried. Kat knew Leva too well. She would do anything to get to Kat.

"Open it," Phil urged, amused.

"Dammit, Phil, stop this," Kat demanded, her fear morphing into anger. "We've got more important work to do here."

Vince shifted his attention to their leader. "Let's not and say we did," he suggested pointedly. "I thought we were through playing games."

Good point, Vince, Kat wanted to say.

All signs of amusement vanished from Phil's expression. "Open it," he repeated icily.

Jamal moved a few steps back, dragging Kat with him. "I think maybe we'll just get outta the way."

Kat tried to wrench free, but he held on tight. "Bastard," she hissed. Jamal only laughed.

Will glanced nervously from Phil to Vince. "Yeah," he muttered, taking a couple of steps away from the threat. "This could get hairy." As an afterthought he rushed back to the table and grabbed his laptop.

Leva watched the whole commotion with obvious glee. "Come on, Ferrelli, don't you want to know what's inside?" she teased.

Kat glared at Leva then at Jamal. "When this is over, I'm going to make you sorry," she warned.

"I tell you what," Vince began nonchalantly, dragging Kat's attention back to him. "Why don't—" before anyone could fathom his intent he threw the box at Phil who barely caught it before it hit the ground. A collective gasp echoed in the silence "—you open it and then I'll take over from there." Vince folded his arms over his chest and smiled. "After all, this is a team thing, right?"

Sheer hatred erupted onto Phil's features, like an earthquake overtaking an unsuspecting village.

Kat's breath caught. "Phil—"

"Of course," Vince interrupted, "if you're afraid, then I can just do it myself."

Without a word, Phil walked to the closest table and placed the package on its surface. He cut one last glance at Vince before slowly tearing away the brown wrapper.

No one moved.

No one spoke.

All eyes focused on Phil's every move.

The paper fell away.

A small pasteboard box remained. The flaps had been tied shut with a piece of twine. Phil untied the string, allowing it to fall on either side of the box.

He pulled the flaps aside.

Phil swore.

He slid the box down the table toward Vince.

Kat's heart surged into her throat.

Years of training and experience under his belt, Vince calmly looked into the open box. A timer ticked down the seconds: 49…48…

Leva thrust a pair of needle-nose pliers in his direction. "You'll need these." She scanned the rest of the group. "I'd move back a little more if I were you."

Vince focused on the nifty little gadget in the box instead of the dispersing group. Forty seconds.

"I hope you've done this before," Leva remarked from right beside him.

Carefully, wasting precious seconds, he lifted the small black device from the box and sat it on the table. Quickly scanning it for access, he raised the plastic lid. A fairly simple configuration of wires, along with a detonator and enough explosive to leave a small crater where he stood were all neatly compacted into the small plastic container.

Clearing his mind of all other stimuli, he focused on the colored wires. One little snip was all it would take, either way. He reached for the most likely one…

Nope. He pulled the tip of the pliers away. It was a decoy.

…20…

He called to mind every wiring schematic he'd ever studied. A line of sweat formed on his brow. This one was incredibly simple…yet there were too many wires.

…15…

"Say the word, Ferrelli," Leva said, leaning toward him to get a look at the timer. "I'll be happy to let you off the hook if you're not up to the challenge."

…10…

A knowing smile slid across his lips. Oh, she was slick.

But not slick enough.

He reached for the wire no bomb-squad tech would touch.

"You sure you want to do that," she said, backing up a step with every word.

Vince snipped the wire.

The timer stopped, two seconds remaining.

Vince tossed the pliers aside took his time assessing Leva. "And you're the best we've got?"

Before Leva could find the voice that no doubt matched the outrage on her face, the rest of the team had crowded around Vince. Kat slid an arm around his waist and scowled at him. "What took you so long?"

"I didn't want to spoil the suspense." He pressed a kiss to her forehead, but he didn't miss the look that passed between Leva and Yu.

Kat had been right. Vince was going to have to watch himself around Yu.

Or he'd be out—feetfirst.

Chapter Six

Vince stood beneath the shower for a long time that night, allowing the hot water to sluice over his tense muscles. He braced himself against the tile, his fingers clenched on the damp surface. He had to find a way to stop tomorrow night's test run. It was far too risky.

He swore. Every swearword he knew in English and a few in half a dozen other languages. He didn't trust Leva. Not one bit, not for a second. Kat would be completely at her mercy inside that building. Vince's post was outside. There would be nothing he could do to help her.

He straightened and swore again.

There had to be a way to stop it.

Defeat surged through him.

And blow his cover in the process.

The water cooled. Vince shut off the spray and grabbed the towel he'd draped over the shower-curtain rod.

He couldn't risk his cover. He knew he couldn't.

Just another reason he should tell Casey this mission

was not salvageable. Let someone else infiltrate WSA at a later time. Dedication to duty poked through the defeat. And how many lives would his selfishness cost? He had no choice but to see this mission through. He knew Kat would do the same in his situation.

The whiz of metal over metal yanked Vince from his worrisome musings.

"My, my, you're a healthy specimen." Leva released the curtain she'd jerked back, but made no offer to turn away. She admired the semi-arousal a hot shower never failed to induce. "I can definitely see why Kat wants to keep you all to herself."

Vince exited the stall, forcing Leva to take a reluctant step back. He slung the towel around his hips and reached for another to swab the water dripping down his face.

"Was there something you wanted?"

She looked him up and down again. "Where shall I start?"

Vince scrubbed the terry cloth down his chest and took his time perusing the femme-fatale-wannabe in front of him. Her black slacks and T-shirt were so tight they looked painted on, which wasn't an entirely bad thing considering her long legs even if she was on the skinny side. In a slutty way, she wasn't that bad to look at. Short, spiky blond hair, brown eyes, nice mouth—as long as it was shut. It was the personality that he found lacking. She cared about no one but herself and had a mean streak a couple miles wide.

"I'll tell you what," Vince said as he folded his arms across his chest. "Why don't you start—" he looked her dead in the eye "—somewhere else since the feeling definitely isn't mutual."

Her face twisted in outrage before she grabbed back control. "A girl can hope," she said, her voice tight despite her clear effort to relax. "Anyway, I just came in here to say good job today."

Vince didn't put much stock in her compliment. "Thanks."

She smiled, one of those deceitful gestures that suggested one thing while meaning another. "Better get some rest tonight. Tomorrow's a big day." She turned and crossed to the door, but hesitated before leaving. "It'll change everything."

When she'd gone, he scrubbed a hand through his damp hair and blew out a breath of frustration. She was right. Tomorrow was the big preview. If Yu and his team successfully pulled off this little demonstration, then the real mission was a go. Tomorrow no one was supposed to die, Yu had assured them. He'd especially emphasized that aspect of the mission to Leva. It was a real-time practice run to make sure they were ready.

It'll change everything.

Leva's final words to Vince had been a clear threat. Maybe no one was supposed to die tomorrow, but every instinct told him that Leva might have other plans.

Vince gathered his clothes and headed to the bedroom he shared with Kat. No way he'd let that psycho hurt Kat. He'd find a way.

He pushed through the bedroom door without knocking, tossed his clothes aside and kicked the door shut behind him. The hiss of a zipper being lowered made Vince realize his mistake. Kat stood at the foot of the bed, her T-shirt tossed aside, her hands at her waist, poised to shove down her unfastened jeans.

An apology shot to the tip of his tongue. He bit it back and resisted the urge to do the gentlemanly thing and turn his back. He wasn't supposed to apologize or to look away. They were a couple. This was normal, though he'd conspicuously avoided the moment for the past twenty-four hours. The memory of how she'd felt in his arms last night made him weak with need.

He couldn't afford weakness.

With a little shimmy that sucked the breath right out of his lungs, she shed the jeans. His gut clenched.

She kicked the jeans aside and reached back to unhook her bra, her spine arching sensually. His gaze zeroed in on the swell of her breasts above their delicate lace cups. He licked his lips like a hungry lion watching its unsuspecting prey.

"Did Leva make a pass at you?" she asked as calmly as if she'd just commented about the current weather conditions.

The question surprised him on a level where he had no control over his ability to reason. Regardless of his failed cognitive processes, he meant to look directly into her eyes when he answered the question, but her next move made that impossible. She shrugged out of the bra.

He'd forgotten how beautiful, how perfect she was. Her small, firm breasts tilted upward, the dusky nipples pebbled as he watched. A slender rib cage narrowed to an incredibly lean waist that, in turn, flared softly into womanly hips. Strappy little pink panties and long, toned legs rendered him speechless for three more seconds.

"What was the question?" He blinked, tried to pull it together. He really did try.

Kat jerked a nightshirt over her head. "Look at me, Vince." Arms folded, jaw set, she marched straight up to him. Those green eyes glittered with anger. "Did she hit on you? I saw her come out of the bathroom. If you were in there—" she gestured to his towel-clad state "—and obviously you were, I want to know if she hit on you."

He wanted to lie. To hold back anything that would increase the animosity between the two women. But lying would only lessen her trust in him. He needed her to trust him.

He braced his hands on his hips and said what had to be said, "Yeah. She did."

Kat looked away, clearly grappling for control.

"I told her to take it elsewhere."

Kat's head came up. She looked far too weary. Dark circles underscored those pretty eyes. "What did she say to that?"

He shrugged. "She pretended she'd only come in to tell me what a good job I'd done earlier."

Seemingly satisfied, Kat padded to the bed, pulled the covers back and crawled beneath them.

Vince frowned. He hadn't relished the idea of a fight, but he hadn't expected disinterest, either. He moved to his side of the bed and sat. "Is something wrong? If you're upset, I'd rather talk about it than let it fester between us."

She didn't even bother to open her eyes and look up at him. Just waved him off, another weary gesture. "I just want to go to sleep—have a headache."

Vince shook his head and battled the need to take her into his arms and get her the hell out of here. What if something was going wrong with the implant? What if the headache was a symptom of something much worse? He was probably the first man in history who hoped I-have-a-headache really meant I'm-avoiding-sex-with-you.

He eased down next to her and pulled her into his arms. She settled against his chest as if she'd spent the last four years that close to his heart…as if things were exactly as they used to be when stolen moments and forbidden passion had ruled their hearts and souls.

"Sleep," he murmured, then pressed a kiss to her forehead. "I'll be right here." He stroked her silky hair and for the first time since his altar boy days, he prayed.

Vince swore to himself right then and there that he would find a way not only to keep her safe but to keep her in his life. He'd let her down four years ago when she'd trusted him on two levels, as an instructor and as a lover. He wouldn't fail her this time—either way.

AT QUARTER OF MIDNIGHT the following night Jamal parked the SUV at the curb on the south side of the block where the International Communications and Securities of Alexandria building was located. For the next fifteen minutes they sat silently waiting. ICS was closed for the night. Business would not resume until nine tomorrow morning. Between now and then, thousands of customers, private citizens as well as businesses and government agencies, counted on electronic security monitored by ICS.

Also on duty inside the building were ten members of night security. The night security base of operations was housed on the first floor, but the guards, two per floor, patrolled the other four floors every hour. Between patrols all personnel remained on the first floor, an indication of the company's confidence in their technology.

But then, they didn't have Will Adams.

Vince had gotten an up-close look at just what Will could do in the simulations he created. The guy was a frigging genius in disguise.

Yu had kept the target a secret from Vince until they were en route. Vince didn't like being unable to warn Lucas, but he'd have to deal with it. Callahan would be passing along their location, but no one would interfere unless it became absolutely necessary. Catching Kovner was far too important. Some sacrifices would have to be made. Vince had been able to pass along the numbers he'd gotten from the scrap of paper in Yu's room. He'd returned the paper hopefully before Yu realized it had been missing.

"Thirty minutes," Yu repeated. "We meet back here in thirty minutes. No exceptions."

Vince glanced at Kat. He liked this less and less every passing minute. He didn't want her going in there without him. He could argue the point…

And blow his cover.

Callahan would be stationed somewhere nearby, but she wouldn't be able to help once Kat was inside.

The entire team was dressed in black cargo pants, combat boots, dark turtlenecks and ski masks. They looked like an assassin squad from an action flick.

"Okay," Yu said with finality. "From this point on we do not speak unless absolutely necessary."

A round of nods acknowledged his order.

Jamal and Will stayed in the SUV. Jamal was the wheelman and general lookout, though no traffic was expected on this street at this hour. According to Yu even the police rarely monitored this block since ICS employed their own top-notch security. Another over-confident assumption.

Will was wired into ICS's security system with a system that rivaled anything Vince had seen the military use. Another indicator of the size of the organization bankrolling this seemingly insignificant group.

After exiting the vehicle, Kat, Leva, Yu and Vince moved through the darkness to the entry point, a rear emergency exit with enough bells and whistles to discourage the best hacker. But not Will. He reveled in the challenge.

A dim light mounted on the exterior wall cast a small pool of light around the wide steel door. Careful to remain beyond the view of the security cameras, they flattened against the wall and waited for the signal.

Right now, as they did every hour on the hour, the guards were patrolling the various floors, checking monitors, and probably chatting about their family problems or the fact that they didn't get paid enough.

At eighteen past the witching hour, Will gave the all-clear signal. As Vince followed the others toward the emergency exit, he heard a hum and then a definitive *click*. The door alarm had just been deactivated.

The exterior security camera as well as the one just inside the door, the one in the stairwell, and all those on the fourth floor were feeding the monitors in the security office the same video play as had been relayed from a quarter of until midnight. Will had recorded the areas during that time of no activity and now he would play that same video on a continuous loop until Leva and Kat were clear. The guards watching the monitors wouldn't see a thing.

Yu opened the door. "Ten minutes. Do not stretch it beyond ten minutes," he reminded them.

Leva and Kat nodded. Vince wanted desperately for Kat to glance in his direction before she went in, but she didn't. The door closed silently behind them. Vince tamped down the urge to go after her. His job was to standby with Yu in case there was any trouble. He had a feeling that it was more a matter of Yu not wanting him out of his sight than of his actually needing Vince.

Following Yu's lead, Vince eased back into the shadows and waited. He closed his eyes and said another quick prayer that Kat would get out safely. That her implant wouldn't choose this moment to go bonkers. That, as Yu had promised, no one would die tonight.

THE SOFT RUBBER SOLES of their shoes were very nearly silent as Kat rushed up the stairs behind Leva.

Two.

The floor number was posted on the outside of the steel door located on each landing they hurried past.

Leva had the silver briefcase containing the designer device they would use to cripple ICS's entire world. This strike held no significance other than as real-time proof of the team's ability, ensuring they were ready for the main event. Tomorrow they would know if they were good enough for a Level Five mission. Few teams received that honor.

Floor three.

Kat skirted the landing in two steps and continued pushing upward. They had practiced long and hard for this—the final proof of their readiness. Her respiration remained steady, her focus undivided. This was a strategic technology hit…nothing more.

No one would be robbed. No top-secret documents would be sucked from government memory banks during the security breach. And no one would be hurt.

Floor four.

"You're still clear," echoed in their earpieces.

Will monitored the real-time feed on the security office and would warn them if the usual protocol was broken. So far, the guards were sticking with the regular routine.

Halfway down the long, wide corridor on the fourth floor a set of double doors protected ICS's elaborate mainframe. Five seconds after reaching the doors, a hum followed by a soft *click* rendered the internal security on the doors useless. But that wasn't the only hurdle. The doors would remain closed until a retinal scan activated the automatic opener.

This was the truly ingenious part of Will's clever plan. Will had entered the ICS system after hours this very day, removed the documented scan belonging to a staff analyst, then replaced it with Leva's. When they were safely back in Port Charlotte, he would undo the change and no one would be the wiser. He would then wipe all traces of his visit from their system. No one would ever know he'd been there.

Leva stepped up to the scanning device and held perfectly still for about two seconds. She smiled when another *click* preceded the automatic opening of the doors.

As soon as the crack between the doors was wide enough, Leva, then Kat, slipped inside the enormous room.

Kat froze.

A stab of pain so fierce she almost blacked out pierced her skull. She squeezed her eyes shut and rode out the worst of it. Leva punched her shoulder to get Kat's attention then pointed to her open case sitting on the tile floor. Leva was ready.

Kat wasn't.

She struggled with the abrupt disorientation. The floor shifted beneath her feet and she felt suddenly sick to her stomach. Something was wrong. She clutched her abdomen.

Leva grabbed Kat by the shoulders and shook her.

The look in her eyes was feral. She pointed to the case again. Kat nodded. She had work to do.

She knelt next to the case.

This wasn't right.

The realization struck her with an intensity that rocked her to the core. Her heart hammered in her chest. Her palms dampened inside her gloves.

She shook it off. Focused on the case. On the device. She had to do this. Phil would kill her if she failed.

Vince.

Vince was waiting for her.

Phil would kill Vince if she failed.

She had to get this done.

Squatting near her, Leva poked Kat in the chest with her forefinger and pointed to her left wrist.

They were running out of time.

Kat had to hurry.

She went to work, ignoring the pain and all the emotions crowding into her brain. She had to focus. She had—she glanced at the timer on the device—six minutes.

Leva, the witch, had already started the countdown.

Two minutes later Kat had the single device strategically located so that it would do the most damage to the mainframe. If it worked like the one they had field tested yesterday, there would be more of an implosion than an explosion.

Kat gave Leva the thumbs-up. They paused long enough at the door for Leva's retinal scan. The doors opened slowly. Leva slipped out first, then Kat.

"You're still clear, ladies."

The reassuring voice in the earpiece eased Kat's anxiety a fraction. Her head wasn't hurting so badly now. She moved swiftly, silently, down the long corridor and into the stairwell.

They had just hit the third-floor landing when Will's voice sounded in Kat's ear again.

"Shit."

Kat jerked to a stop. "What?" she demanded in a hushed whisper.

Leva shook her head and motioned for her to keep moving.

"We've got a uniform on the fourth floor. Just stepped off the elevator and looks like he's headed to the supply room."

Kat's blood ran cold.

"He's too close to the blast zone," Will warned. "He'll eat it when she blows."

No one is supposed to die.

Kat wheeled around and lunged up the stairs.

"Get back here," Leva snarled.

Kat ignored her.

Leva rushed up behind her, grabbed her by the arm.

Kat reached for her weapon as she twisted around to face her. She shoved the weapon beneath Leva's stubborn chin. "I will not let that man die. Now get the hell out of here and let me do what I have to do."

Leva released her. "It's your funeral." She turned and resumed her descent.

"Give me his twenty," Kat demanded.

"Twenty? What the hell is that?" Will shouted in her

ear. "You'd better get outta there. That thing is going to blow in just over two minutes."

"Where's the damned guard?" Kat burst into the corridor, her weapon drawn, her stance battle ready.

"He's in the damn supply closet!"

"What the hell is going on?"

Yu's voice.

Kat disregarded the question.

The supply room door stood wide open. She eased around it. The guard reached toward the top shelf for a sleeve of foam coffee cups, of all things. The guy was going to die because he wanted a lousy cup of coffee.

He was too big to drag, so she couldn't knock him unconscious. She silently cursed her bad luck.

Kat had his gun from his holster before he even knew she was standing right behind him.

"Don't move," she warned, nudging the barrel of the forty-caliber weapon into his kidneys. "We have to get out of here. This place is going to blow."

"In one minute fifty," Will supplied nervously.

"What do you think you're doing, lady?" the guard demanded, his hands high in the air.

"Saving your butt," she growled. She grabbed him by the back of his belt and backed him out of the supply room. "We're going down the stairwell. We need to hurry."

He finally moved forward when she jabbed the muzzle of the weapon a little deeper into his flesh.

"You won't get away with this," he threatened. "I don't know how you got in here…"

Whatever else he said was drowned out by Yu's heated command in Kat's ear. "Get out now or we leave without you." She didn't miss the slight tremor in his voice.

"On my way," she muttered. "Open the door," she instructed the guard. When he didn't, she reached around him. He made his move. She had no choice. She put him down with the right pressure on just the right spot on his neck.

"Idiot," she muttered.

"One minute," Will warned. "Get out, Kat. Get out now."

"Doing that as we speak." She groaned with the effort of dragging the guard through the stairwell door and across the fourth-floor landing. She tugged him down the stairs. The going was slow, but at least they were moving downhill and away from the danger. He would be as sore as hell tomorrow, but at least he'd be alive.

Leva burst through the emergency exit and into the back alley. "That stupid bitch is dragging the guard down the stairs."

Yu swore.

"Forty seconds," Will announced.

Outright panic hit Vince low in the gut. He couldn't wait any longer. He shoved Leva away from the door. "I'm going in to help her."

The muzzle of Yu's weapon jammed into Vince's right temple. "No you're not. We're leaving. She has less than one minute to return or we leave without her. We're not hanging around for the show."

Vince's response to Yu's order was anatomically impossible. He jerked the door open and bolted up the stairs, leaving Yu to do what he would.

The blast shook the building just as Vince hit the second-floor landing. He grabbed the railing for balance and kept going. The scene on the third-floor landing paralyzed him. Kat lay sprawled in an awkward position; the guard a few feet away, his body draped down the lower portion of the stairs.

The sound of an alarm going off jolted Vince back into action. He checked Kat's pulse. She was alive. Thank God. The breath he'd been holding rushed from his lungs. He prayed nothing was broken. They had to get out of here. He quickly ran his hands along her torso and limbs. With nothing else to do, he gently lifted her into his arms. Fear banded around his chest when she hung like a limp rag doll.

He started down the stairs, then remembered the guard. Kat would want to know that he was all right. Vince reached through the railing and checked his pulse, strong and steady.

Taking the stairs two at a time with Kat held firmly against his chest, Vince sprinted through the rear exit without being spotted. He had the sudden urge to cross himself in thanks, but he'd have to do that later.

Yu and Leva were nowhere in sight. Vince glanced right then left in the dark alley and made his decision. He'd go back to the rendezvous point on the off chance they hadn't left just yet.

When he reached the south side of the block, Vince was stunned to find the black SUV waiting at the very end of the block. Breathing hard, but determined not to let up, Vince ran the whole way, Kat clutched against him.

Will opened the back door and jumped out to help get Kat inside. "I didn't think you guys were going to make it."

For the first time since they'd met, Vince saw the fear in the kid's eyes.

"Let's go," Yu ordered before Vince was all the way inside the vehicle.

Vince flung himself onto the seat and pulled the door shut as Jamal went from zero to sixty in record time.

Vince pulled Kat back into his lap. He carefully removed her ski mask. Blood trickled from her hairline just beneath her right ear.

He breathed a curse. "We need a hospital," he said hoarsely.

Leva shouted from the cargo seat, "Are you insane? We can't go to a hospital. Just shoot her and dump her somewhere."

"This is wack!" Jamal shouted. "I ain't going—"

Fury erupted inside Vince. He pulled his weapon and bored it deeply into the back of the driver's skull. "Take me to a hospital. *Now.*" He barely recognized the primal, savage voice as his own.

"No way," Yu said. "We'll take care of her."

Vince cocked his weapon. "I said—"

Yu reached over the seat, his own weapon aimed at Kat. "Put the weapon away, Ferrelli. We'll handle the situation."

"No one was supposed to die," Will screamed from the cargo seat.

"Shut up!" Leva screamed back at him.

"Lower your weapon now," Yu ordered. "Or medical attention will be the last thing she needs."

Vince relented. He struggled to control the shaking rampant in his body. Kat was still unconscious. Vince looked from her to Yu who had shifted his aim from Kat to Vince and looked ready to give him a third eye and a ticket straight to hell.

Vince leveled a look on Yu that made him flinch. "If she dies, you're finished."

Chapter Seven

Kat clawed her way out of the darkness. The pain in her head almost overpowered her, dragging her back downward. She fought it. Someone called her name—wanted her to wake up…

Vince.

She let the sound of his voice guide her until her eyes opened. A bright light shone in her face. She flinched, squeezed her eyes shut. "The light," she muttered.

The answering *click* was comforting.

"Talk to me, baby," Vince urged, his voice unsteady, wrought with fear.

A "Thank God" echoed from somewhere. Sounded like Will's voice. Then, "I told you fools that you couldn't kill the Kat woman." *Jamal.* "She's prob'ly got nine lives."

She tried to sit up. Another shaft of pain seared through her skull.

"Take it easy." Vince again. "You got a pretty good knock on the head. I really need to get a good look in your eyes. You up to dealing with the light?"

"Yeah," she murmured, some part of her aware that he was right. If she had a concussion, she needed to know it.

Vince shone the intense light first in one eye and then the other. Kat paid the price. For long seconds after she squeezed her lids tightly together the harsh starburst still glowed like the noonday sun.

"Responses are good," he said softly. His relief was palpable.

Only then did Kat become aware of the subtle rocking motion. They were moving. She concentrated hard to get her bearings. Vince held her in his lap, his strong arms keeping her close to his chest. She could feel the steady beat of his heart. A weary sigh seeped past her lips. She was safe. The pain had lessened. Vince would take care of her—

The guard…

"What about the guard?" she demanded, her eyes wide open now, the fog clearing a bit.

"He was out cold but breathing," Vince assured her. "No visible injuries."

"Next time you do something that stupid," Leva growled from the back seat, "I'm going to shoot you myself. You could have gotten us both killed. It wasn't enough you got all freaky during the job."

A surge of anger burned off the last of the haze enveloping her. Kat sat up straighter, looking past Vince's shoulder to make eye contact with Leva. Vince restrained her with those powerful arms when she would have tried to break free of his hold. Kat had only one thing on her mind: getting to the heartless witch in the cargo seat. She squirmed in his hold. Her head spun. Defeated, she sagged against Vince, held her head in her hands to slow its spinning. It didn't work.

"No sudden moves for a while," he cautioned.

"We'll settle this later," Kat warned Leva.

Phil turned toward Kat, his fierce glare visible in the dim glow from the dash display. "This discussion is over."

His fleeting glance in Kat's direction hadn't lessened in its ferocity, but she didn't miss the flare of concern it contained.

Kat slumped against Vince. She didn't have the strength to argue with Leva right now anyway. And analyzing Phil's concern under the circumstances definitely required more brainpower than she possessed at the moment. She closed her eyes and surrendered to her body's desperate need for rest. They would know by dawn if their mission had been successful.

Vince would take care of her now.

That was all she needed to know.

VINCE WATCHED Kat sleep. She looked so damned fragile. He gritted his teeth against the string of profanities that burgeoned in his chest. He'd done a hell of a job keeping her safe. He turned away from the bed and stared out the window. He'd failed. He closed his eyes and called himself every kind of fool for allowing this completely insane mission to continue.

Images from four years ago flashed one after the other through his mind. The feel of her skin…the taste of her lips. The heat that exploded between them with all the force of a nuclear blast.

He'd let her down then, too.

Vince forced his eyes open and sucked in a shuddering breath. Why was it that he could never do anything right where Kat was concerned? He shook his head. Because he hadn't realized then what he realized now. What they'd shared was far more important than anything else, even his career. He'd made a mistake; she would never forgive him.

As soon as she remembered what he couldn't forget, it would be over…forever.

He glanced at his watch to see if it was time to rouse her again. Though he was reasonably sure from her physical responses that she didn't have a concussion, he knew from his medic training that he should wake her every hour.

He'd cleaned and bandaged the small tear in her scalp. It wasn't large or deep, just bled a lot, as did all head injuries. Scared the hell out of him mostly. He'd examined the rest of her more thoroughly once he'd gotten her into bed. No other injuries were apparent. She wasn't even sore…that would come in a few hours.

The night grayed into dawn while he watched, lost in thought. ICS had no doubt spent the last several hours scrambling to divert their operations to an alternate mainframe, something they should have thought of long ago. Vince hoped like hell that there were no secondary motives for this particular little sideshow. The best he could guess was that it represented two things. First, proof that Yu's team could make the kind of strategic maneuver the WSA wanted. Second, that no kind of security system was safe from their reach.

He imagined that the WSA had scored a hit on both agendas. They'd sent a bold message to anyone smart enough to listen: we're here and we can do this with a ragtag team handpicked from the most ordinary walks of life.

Apprehension lit in Vince's gut. The mission he'd watched go down at midnight had convinced him of one thing if nothing else, a terrorist could do anything if the people he surrounded himself with were motivated enough. Even scarier was the idea of how many kids out there were potential replicas of Will Adams. Cyber security was going to have to go to a whole new level if the world was to ever be safe again.

Too many young people were looking for something or someone to make them feel as if they belonged. Philip Yu was a perfect example. As were Jamal Johnson and Will Adams. Leva, well, she was just a psycho. Vince didn't know the full story on her. But he doubted she had any higher aspirations of making the world a better place or leaving her mark. She just liked to blow things up. The WSA had given her the means to do that. But the others had stronger motivation, they were convinced this would make them heroes in the end.

Vince glanced at Kat. No matter what the implant forced her to believe about herself, the compassionate woman he'd known four years ago was still there. She risked her life to save that security guard. He doubted any of the others would have done it. Maybe Will. He'd sounded upset when he realized the guy had entered the danger zone.

"Hey."

Vince turned at the sound of Kat's tentative voice. She'd pushed up from her pillows, braced herself on her elbows and was studying him as if he was the patient instead of her.

He smiled, so damned relieved that she was okay. "Hey, yourself."

"Come over here, Ferrelli." She patted the covers beside her. When he'd settled next to her, she looked into his eyes and said, "I'm okay. Don't beat yourself up. You didn't do anything wrong. So stop looking all guilty."

Man, he was about as transparent as glass. He cupped her face, stroked her cheek with his thumb, reveling in the feel of her soft skin. "You scared the hell out of me."

She sat up and looped her arms around his neck. "That was just payback for staying gone so long this time."

Vince didn't care what anyone said. His gut told him that part of what she said was real. Somewhere deep inside her she knew he'd done her wrong. Though she didn't realize the depth of his betrayal, she sensed the transgression.

He closed his eyes and gently rested his forehead against hers. "I am so sorry, Kat." His voice shook just a little, but he didn't care. "I wish I could go back and make it right. But I can't." He pulled back to look at her. He searched her emerald-colored eyes, his heart reacting to their sheer beauty and the infinite trust he saw there. "Promise me that you won't ever forget how sorry I am for—"

She pressed a finger to his lips, traced the nearly healed injury he'd incurred what felt like a lifetime ago now.

"Don't say any more, Vince," she whispered. "It doesn't matter." A watery smile trembled across her lips, pooled in her eyes. "All that matters is here and now."

He fought the need and desire attempting to overpower his ability to reason. "Whatever happens," he insisted, "never forget that I know how wrong I was."

"I won't." She nipped his lower lip with her teeth, sending a spear of heat straight to his loins. "Now kiss me, tough guy, before you say something that'll dispel that image entirely."

Kat didn't have to ask twice. Vince kissed her slowly, gently. She wanted more. Tugging his T-shirt from his jeans, she pushed it upward and off, her mouth going right back to his without missing a beat. Her hands splayed over his bare skin and she moaned. He felt so good.

Smooth, hot skin stretched tautly over rippling muscles. Strength vibrated along every inch of his sculpted frame. Desire coiled beneath her belly button. She wanted him to touch her the way she was touching him. Instantly his hands molded to her sides, as if he'd read her mind. Those strong hands slid over the cotton of her nightshirt, pausing to cup the weight of her unrestrained breasts. Pleasure cascaded through her.

One thumb stroked across her nipple. She whimpered, his skilled mouth drinking in the sound. His tongue, sleek and hot, thrust inside at the same time that his fingers tightened around her breasts. Desire burst like a fireworks display, showering her with sparks of heat. She arched her back, jutting her breasts into his palms, a wordless plea for more. He leaned her back into the fluffy pillows, his kiss growing more intense, more possessive.

She melted in his arms, his hands tracing her body, hers doing the same to his. There wasn't a man alive who could kiss like Vince Ferrelli. He'd sworn that he'd honed his technique at the tender age of eleven behind a tree on the school playground in Trenton, New Jersey. She didn't care where he'd developed the skill, only that he was using it on her now.

She pulled him closer, needing the feel of his chest against her tingling breasts. He withdrew slightly from the kiss, just enough so they could catch their breaths.

"I need to be inside you," he murmured breathlessly against her hungry lips.

Kat wanted to weep with joy. "Please," she urged, lifting her hips to meet the hand sliding down to where she ached so desperately for his touch. But a mere touch would never be enough.

His lips made a path along her jaw, the curve of her neck, and then downward…toward her breasts. Those magic fingers of his slipped inside her panties, touched her most intimate feminine flesh. Her breathing rapid and shallow, her own fingers dug into his muscled shoulders.

An insistent pounding on the door stalled the penetrating touch her body needed. Now!

Refusing to be drawn from this place of sweet sensation, Kat placed a restraining hand on his when he would have pulled away. "No. I don't want you to stop."

The pounding came again. "Downstairs. *Now.*" The curtly issued order was punctuated by expectant silence.

Kat wanted to scream in frustration. "We have to get dressed," she huffed.

Vince took his time, seeming to memorize every little detail of her face, before his gaze connected with hers. Those gray eyes were dark, molten with desire. "Later," he promised, then kissed her again. So soundly, so sweetly, that she lost her breath all over again.

When he stood and turned away from her, something about that broad, muscular back and the way his jeans fit his perfect butt sparked a memory. Just a flash of that amazing body clothed in nothing but camouflage fatigue pants riding low on his hips and a single promise-filled word…*later.*

Kat was still reeling from the memory ten minutes after as Phil paced back and forth in the living room. Everyone sat, waiting for him to begin.

It was 8:00 a.m. Time enough to have received feedback from their strike, she supposed. They'd done everything right. The only glitch was her having to rescue that guard. And even that little deviation was acceptable, in her opinion, since Phil had reiterated over and over that no one was supposed to die. There was no reason to suspect the mission was a failure.

Will had spent the entire ten minutes she and Vince had been waiting setting up what looked like a conferencing system on the scarred Formica dining table. Restless, Kat studied her surroundings and tried to compare it to places she'd lived before, to where she'd grown up.

Nothing came.

She frowned.

Why couldn't she call to mind her last home? Or even where it had been located? She had a vague impression of the general area around D.C., but nothing concrete. How could she remember Vince's grade-school antics and not her own? The distant yet perpetual throb deep in the back of her skull nagged at her, insinuating something she should understand but didn't.

Fear crept into her heart…made her cold. Something was very, very wrong with her. She regarded Vince, who looked blatantly indifferent to Phil's growing agitation. Maybe she should tell him just how deep her problems went….

Fear swept through her. No, she couldn't do that. She had no intention of doing anything that would send him away again. That vague image of him in military fatigues filtered through her thoughts again. She hadn't known Vince in the military…had she? Had he even been in the military?

She blinked away the unbidden image and turned her attention to Phil. Jamal and Leva had grown impatient. Jamal drummed his fingers against the arm of his chair; Leva kept shifting from one position to the other. Phil continued to pace. Kat examined her own feelings. She was calm. Sore as hell, but calm. Her only impatience was with her mind's insistent wandering to questions she couldn't answer. She glanced at the man beside her once more. He was definitely calm. If he were anymore so, he'd be dead.

Why didn't either of them feel anxious about the coming postmortem? She had certainly broken protocol; she should at least be worried about taking a hit for that. Vince had done the same. She had no explanation.

Kat sighed and pushed the troubling thoughts away.

Phil stopped and turned at the sound of her heavy exhale. "Are you bored?"

He didn't have to address her by name, he looked straight at her. "Do you care?" she snapped right back.

Jamal leaned forward and braced his thick forearms on his widespread knees. "Maybe he's just wondering how you could be bored considering you're lucky as hell to be breathing."

"And maybe—" Phil sent a look in Jamal's direction that cut to the bone "—I can speak for myself."

Jamal muttered a stinging expletive, which Phil chose to ignore.

"When this—" he nodded to the system Will had just finished preparing "—is done, *we* will talk."

Kat felt Vince's tension escalate; to his credit, he kept his mouth shut.

"All set," Will announced when Phil finally stopped glaring at Kat.

Phil nodded curtly. He strode to the table and punched in a series of numbers. When the call was answered on the second ring, Phil didn't wait for a greeting. "Philip Yu here, sir."

A chill sliced through Kat. It was him. The guy

Jamal was always calling The Man. She didn't have to hear his voice and no one had to tell her. She felt it. A foreboding uneasiness settled in the pit of her stomach. She tried to shake it, but it refused to vacate her senses.

This wasn't right.

She'd had that overwhelming premonition just before she placed the device at ICS. It still nagged at her.

"Well done, Mr. Yu." The voice was heavy, gravelly, with no inflection at all. Not real. Distorted.

The Man was using a device to alter his voice. She was suddenly as certain of that as she was her own name.

"Your team has surpassed our expectations."

"Thank you, sir."

Kat looked from one member of the team to the other. All listened intently, leaning forward in their seats as if that posture would help them to hear better…to discern something from that disguised voice beyond the prepared words he spoke. Vince sat completely still, his expression intent, as well. But there was something different about his demeanor. He wasn't anticipating the pat on the back the rest of them panted for. Vince was absorbing and analyzing what he heard.

Her gaze then sought Phil. He stood at attention, his expression filled with pride yet somehow humbled. This was the moment he'd waited for his entire life.

Kat simply listened, almost as if she knew what was to come. As if…she'd long anticipated it and knew exactly what to do. But how could she?

"In three days we will cut out a cancer that has continued to grow right under the noses of those whom we count on to keep us secure."

A heavy pause permeated the room for a time. This was the moment they'd all waited for. The team would move to the next level.

"You have your instructions, Mr. Yu."

"Yes, sir."

A *click* signaled the call had been ended.

Phil said to Leva, "You have seventy-two hours. Will you be ready?"

"I'll be ready in forty-eight," she tossed back. "Less if necessary," she added in that haughty, overconfident tone that grated on Kat's nerves.

He turned to Will then. "And you?"

Will shrugged. "No problemo. I downloaded the new schematics this morning. I'll start working on it now." He pushed up and sauntered upstairs to his room.

Jamal glanced at Kat suspiciously then glared at Phil. "Is everybody in on this 'cept me?"

Kat flared her hands. "Don't feel slighted, J-Man. I don't know any more than what we've just heard."

Vince said nothing.

Everyone in the room knew he was uninformed. If he was miffed by it, it didn't show.

"You'll know what you need to when the time comes," Phil told Jamal pointedly.

"I got class." Jamal pushed to his feet. "You got my number." He stormed out of the house.

Phil turned his attention to Kat then. "We have to talk." He slid a sideways glance at Vince. *"Alone."*

Vince's jaw tightened visibly. He stood, his gaze never leaving Phil. "I guess I'll take a walk." He touched Kat's cheek, his intent glare lingering on Phil, then left.

When the door had closed Phil pressed Leva with a look that said "Get lost."

Not quite as dense as she was stubborn, Leva got up. "I guess I'll go play in the basement." Her shop. A bomb lover's wet dream. Kat avoided the place like the plague.

After Leva left, Kat stood, evening up the playing field. She folded her arms over her chest and met Phil's scrutiny. "Give it to me straight, Phil. I don't want to play games here."

He moved closer to her, as if what he had to say was too confidential to allow it to cross that much air space. "*He* doesn't like it. This is supposed to be a five-man team."

Kat lifted one shoulder in a careless shrug. "Then we're screwed anyway. Maybe you haven't noticed, but I'm not a man. The verdict is still out on Leva."

His fierce gaze softened the tiniest fraction. "You know I've noticed."

Tension vibrated between them for one second that lapsed into five.

"I know," she relented. "And you know how I feel."

He looked away. "He's not the right man for you, Kat."

"And you are?" She put a hand on his arm. She did like Phil. Just not the way he wanted her to. "We're friends, Phil. Good friends. Let's not lose that. Our mission is too important."

Phil closed his eyes, his expression pained. Kat didn't

want to hurt him, but she was in love with Vince. Her heart went out to this strong man who struggled so hard to make his mark. He worked harder than any of them.

"We don't need Ferrelli." Phil looked at her now, his expression carefully composed once more. "But I will allow him to remain on one condition."

A twinge of trepidation twisted inside her. "Name it."

"If I prove beyond all doubt that he is using you to try and stop this mission—"

"Then I'm dead," Kat interjected, tamping down the anxiety climbing into her throat. "I know that."

He shook his head. "If I'm right about Ferrelli, then you belong to me." His eyes held hers in a vise of anticipation. "In every sense of the word."

VINCE WALKED in the direction of the marina for several minutes before Callahan appeared. She stood at the corner of a bait-and-tackle shop reading the newspaper. He turned toward the shop but walked right past it, heading into the alley that separated it from the marina office. Callahan followed.

He hadn't wanted to leave Kat, but this might be his only opportunity to slip away without being followed. Passing along the intel he had so far was essential. And maybe she'd have something on that sequence of numbers.

"Got something for me, Ferrelli?"

She leaned against the rustic wood wall of the bait shop, opened her paper once more and feigned interest in the classifieds.

"It's going down in three days." Vince continually

scanned the area. The far end of the alley was a dead end, the back of another building butted firmly against it. At the other end was the street where they'd entered. There weren't any pedestrians out since it was still early; any interested in fishing were already on the water.

"We're going to need a few more details," she said facetiously, shooting him a look over the top of the paper. Those extraordinary blue eyes flashed with amusement.

"Will has the schematics of the target downloaded. But Yu is keeping the details to himself for the moment. They'll do a simulated walk-through, I'm sure of it." Vince leaned against the opposite wall. "As soon as I have anything, I'll find a way to pass it along. Keep your eyes open. I may not get this kind of chance next time. What about those numbers?" he asked as an afterthought.

"A bank account in the Caymans. They're tracing the owner now. All bets are on Kovner." Callahan quirked an eyebrow. "And how's your lady friend?"

"A little banged up, but okay." Vince frowned, worry eating at him again. "She's having some problems. Side effects from the implant, I'm thinking. Headaches and distorted memories. Maybe even a little paranoia, definitely some confusion. Ask Lucas to check into that. I need to know if there are specific warning signs to watch for. If she's going to have some sort of meltdown, I need to be prepared."

That was a lie. If the risk was increasing, he wanted to get her out. End of story. His chest constricted with worry.

Callahan folded the newspaper and tucked it under her arm. "Everything else under control?"

Vince nodded. Another lie. If he and Yu lasted the next seventy-two hours without killing each other it would be a miracle.

She read the lie as easily as she had the local headlines. "I've been watching Yu's body language when the two of you are together." She shook her head. "He's going to try to take you out of the picture. I think he's more hung up on Kat than we anticipated."

Vince rubbed a hand over his unshaven face. "He'll try." Vince was tired. Tired and seriously worried about Kat.

"I can only watch your back when you're in the open, Ferrelli. You need to be very careful. I've got a really bad feeling about this guy."

Vince considered her words. "Leva's the one we need to worry about," he argued. "She's nuts." He thought about the way she'd interrupted his shower. "She might do anything." She posed a serious threat to Kat, as well.

Callahan pushed off the building. "That's true enough, but the deal with Yu goes much deeper. This is a guy whose been searching for something his whole life. He thinks he's found it in WSA and with Kat. You threaten that. He could be more dangerous than you think."

"Thanks for the insight, but I can handle Yu." Vince gave her a little two-fingered salute. "Until next time."

Blue Callahan watched Vince Ferrelli walk away. He was in deep trouble here. This mission was far too personal. He didn't just have a past with Katrina Moore, he was in love with the woman. Blue had never been in love herself but she could recognize the symptoms a mile away. She'd watched her five brothers take that sometimes painful journey.

Vince had it bad. The problem was, so did Philip Yu. They were in love with the same woman, which made them mortal enemies on a much deeper level than simply being on opposite sides of the law.

Vince was too sure of himself.

He was convinced he had everything under control.

That kind of confidence was dangerous.

Chapter Eight

"Phil, you can't expect me to—"

He shook his head, his eyes flashing a warning, his expression grim. "Don't say anything you'll regret."

Kat's heart started to pound, but it had more to do with fear for Vince than anticipation of what Phil might intend for her, now or later. She wasn't afraid of him...not like that. Not really.

"Are you prepared to agree to this condition?"

He was closer now, his entire body seeking, urging a response from hers. Only slightly taller than she, he peered down at her with such intensity that he seemed to tower over her, demanding her attention...her submission.

She couldn't give him what he wanted.

The man in charge didn't like the idea of Vince on the team, but he would leave the final say up to Phil. Phil was willing to stand by his original decision to allow Vince in, *if* she agreed to his one condition.

It would be a simple thing really. But it frightened her unreasonably. On a level she couldn't quite comprehend, she knew that not much had ever scared her…this scared her. To Phil, a person's word was everything. Once she gave it, there was no taking it back.

She met Phil's relentless gaze with a determined one of her own. "Of course. I'm always prepared for anything. You know that."

"Then we have a deal."

She nodded, apprehension knotting in her stomach.

He reached for her.

She didn't dare pull away for fear of what that transgression would cost Vince. Her fingers curled into tight fists of resistance at her sides.

Phil's hands—fingers long, palms rough from hard work—closed around her throat and drew her mouth up to meet his.

Kat shivered with trepidation, a gasp escaping.

His eyes closed as their lips touched. She felt him tremble as he settled into the kiss. His mouth was hungry for her, desperate to evoke the desired reaction.

Every fiber of her being screamed at her to pull away, but her mind held her paralyzed. If she denied him this and he did anything to endanger Vince—

The front door opened.

Frozen like a wild animal caught in the high beams, Kat could only pray that it was Jamal who'd walked in as Phil set her away from him.

He licked his lips and glanced toward the door. The smug look that claimed his features gave her the answer before she even turned around.

Vince.

She knew no words to accurately describe the blood-thirsty rage on his face.

His murderous gaze fixed on Phil, his fists clenched, Vince strode toward them. Phil leaped onto the couch then over the back, landing right in front of Vince, weapon drawn.

Kat's heart shuddered. She reached for her weapon and came up empty. She'd left it on the table by the bed. Her gaze swung to the staircase. There wasn't time.

"You have something to say, Ferrelli?" Phil asked, his smile cocksure as he leveled his bead right between Vince's eyes, not three inches from his forehead.

Vince didn't return the smile. "You'd better kill me, you son of a bitch, because you're dead."

Kat lost her breath. She had to do something.

"Stop," she demanded, her heart racing as she moved toward the two men facing off in the middle of the room.

"Stay out of this," Vince growled, not even sparing her so much as a glance. "This time it's between him and me."

Fury evaporated most of Kat's fear. Men! What arrogant fools. She turned her attention to Phil. "Put the gun down. We had a deal, remember?" She hoped like hell this would work. All the excitement was making her head hurt worse.

Vince's attention jerked in her direction. "What kind of deal?" he roared.

She sighed wearily. "Give it a rest, Vince. It wasn't what it looked like," she urged, her nerves frazzled. She didn't need this crap.

"Wasn't it?" he demanded, his voice too loud.

He was way beyond reason. She saw the battle taking place inside him, saw him tremble with the effort of hanging on to a single shred of control.

"It's none of your business," Phil said flatly. "That's what it was."

"Phil, please," she pleaded. "Put your gun away. We have less than seventy-two hours on the clock. There's no time for this."

Phil's stance wavered. Hesitantly he lowered the weapon. "For you," he told her, his eyes relaying the truth in his words. "Only for you."

This was way, way out of control.

"Big mistake, friend," Vince said with such animosity that Kat flinched.

Vince had his weapon drawn, aimed directly at Phil's heart.

Kat swore. Perfect.

"You're the one making the mistake, Ferrelli," Phil said calmly.

Kat shook her head and threw up her arms. She'd had enough. "Fine. You two go ahead and kill each other." She marched over to the door, grabbed the keys to the SUV and snatched up the backpack she'd deserted there two days ago. "I'm out of here."

She had a class anyway. She'd already missed one this term, no point pushing her luck where her grade point average was concerned. She slammed the door behind her.

To hell with men.

Vince blinked.

He couldn't believe she'd walked out.

Some of the fire went out of his outrage.

He swore, an ugly, self-deprecating phrase.

Yu lifted one dark eyebrow. "That was good, Ferrelli. Now she's gone. Do you always have this effect on women?"

"Shut up." He gifted Yu with a drop-dead glare.

"Are you going to shoot me or what?"

Oh, he wanted to, all right. It was all Vince could do not to do just that.

Yu laughed. "I didn't think so."

"If you ever touch her again," Vince told him, his anger kicking into incineration mode again, "I swear I'll kill you." His fingers tightened on the weapon in his hand. The need to finish this now was very nearly overpowering.

The standoff lasted several more seconds before Vince reluctantly lowered his weapon and shoved it back into his waistband. Kat had taken off. He had to find her. He turned his back on Yu—in spite of the knowledge that the guy wanted to kill him—and strode toward the door.

"You won't win, Ferrelli."

Vince turned back and allowed him to see the complete confidence he felt. "I'll win. And when I do, I'll make sure you're around to watch."

Yu smirked. "She's already mine. You just don't know it yet."

Vince stabbed a finger in his direction. "This isn't finished." Then he walked out. It was either that or kill the smug SOB. He straddled his motorcycle and revved the engine. He forced Yu's words from his mind. Yu would not win.

Kat belonged to Vince.

IT DIDN'T TAKE Vince long to locate Kat. He'd memorized her class schedule. He waited on the portico as he had the last time. He'd spent an hour and a half chastising himself for acting like a fool. He'd let his temper get the better of him. There had to be a reasonable explanation for what happened, he was certain of it. Kat and Yu had been alone. He'd likely taken advantage of her. After all, she was pretty shaken from last night's adventure.

She's already mine. You just don't know it yet.

Vince refused to lend any credence to that claim. He'd watched Yu and Kat together. The attraction was solely one-sided. A little voice playing devil's advocate made him consider that the two had been working together for an entire month before Vince came into the picture.

He remembered something Kat had said that first day. *You disappear for weeks, leaving me to my own devices.* Maybe there had been something more than Vince wanted to acknowledge between them…temporarily. She'd admitted a mild attraction.

What was he thinking? Until the implant kicked in, she hadn't even known Vince might be coming. There had been absolutely no legitimate reason for her not to get involved with Yu. That could explain the rest of the team's antagonism toward her.

Vince shook his head. He wasn't going there. He had no right to be jealous of the life Kat had led since they'd parted ways. He'd certainly done his share of carousing around. How the hell could he hold her accountable?

He couldn't.

Callahan was right. She knew Vince was too close to this to be objective. That was the motivation behind today's little pep talk. She saw what was right in front of his face.

Yu was playing him.

Vince rubbed at the tension knotting the back of his neck. He'd have to find a way to discuss this with Kat without losing it. That wasn't going to be easy. Every time he thought about Yu touching her he went berserk.

He loosened his shoulders and started to pace. Anything to work off some of the adrenaline.

A flash of navy blue and coppery curls against white snagged his attention. Kat's backpack was navy blue and she'd worn a white T-shirt and khaki slacks. He started after her, had taken a breath to call her name, but something stopped him.

She moved purposely toward the lot where she'd parked the SUV. A few steps back, but definitely keeping pace with her was a man. Forty maybe, three-piece suit, wire-rimmed eyeglasses. Vince considered that he could simply be one of the professors at the school headed to the parking area, as well.

But that wasn't the case. There was something about the way this guy moved. Something watchful. Predatory, though obviously uncaring of who might notice his stalking.

Vince moved toward his bike, careful to keep both Kat and the guy under surveillance.

Kat drove out of the parking lot. The suit got into a nondescript gray sedan and followed her.

Vince did the same, staying two cars behind the gray sedan.

Callahan would be around somewhere. He didn't bother looking for her. She was too good at making herself invisible. As were all Specialists.

The drive from the campus to the house Yu had rented six months ago took only fifteen minutes. Kat pulled into the drive. The gray sedan slowed but drove on past. The guy was definitely following Kat.

Vince tailed the sedan. The man drove a couple blocks then took a right. Three blocks later, in a quiet neighborhood, a traffic signal turned red, forcing the car to stop.

Vince rocked his bike onto the kickstand, hopped off and strode straight up to the car. He wrenched the door open before the man even knew he was there.

"What the hell?" he asked, startled.

Ignoring the question, Vince forced the gearshift into Park and jerked the guy out. He pinned him face-first against the hood and shoved the nose of his 9 mm into the base of his skull. "Who the hell are you?" Vince demanded.

While the guy stammered for an answer, Vince scanned the neighborhood for any signs of movement. He didn't need anyone calling the cops about a gunman in the street.

"I'm…I'm Russ Damrus."

Vince leaned closer, grinding the words out right in

the guy's ear. "That doesn't tell me a damned thing. Now, who the hell are you? And why are you following Katrina Moore?"

"Who?" Sweat beaded on the man's pale forehead.

Vince went deadly still, his voice softened dangerously low. "Don't lie to me. I don't want to have to waste you right here."

"Okay! Okay! I'm with the CIA."

Vince's blood ran cold. He felt for the guy's wallet. He tugged it out and checked the ID. He muttered an expletive.

"You've seen the ID, now let me up before I…before I arrest you!" Damrus wailed.

Vince almost laughed as he patted the guy down with one hand while keeping the weapon tucked against his brain stem with the other. "Where's your piece?" He should have recognized the suit…the pathetic surveillance technique.

"It's in the car. Under the seat," Damrus sputtered. "I don't go into the classroom armed."

Classroom?

Vince jerked the guy up and turned him around. "What the hell are you doing in Port Charlotte?"

Damrus swallowed hard. "I'm…I'm keeping an eye on Katrina."

Vince struggled to keep his respiration calm and his temper even. "Under whose authorization?"

Damrus's expression turned indignant. "Who the hell are you?"

The look Vince adopted made the guy recoil in fear.

"You don't want to know the answer to that. Now tell me why you're here." If Damrus was CIA and working this case, wouldn't he know who Vince was? Maybe not. Those guys worked a lot of black ops where the phrase "need to know" was carried to the extreme.

Damrus held up his hands. "You're right. I don't want to know. I arranged for one of Katrina's professors to take leave so that I could keep an eye on her."

Vince narrowed his gaze. "Why?"

"I'm…" Damrus swallowed again. "I'm the man who designed the implant. I've been monitoring her condition as best I could since she went dark."

Dark. That was CIA jargon for *incommunicado*. The very idea that the CIA would put a man this close to Kat, especially one who didn't know jack about undercover work or the ongoing op, infuriated Vince.

"Who authorized this?" he demanded again.

Damrus let go a shaky breath. "No one. I'm supposed to be on vacation. I was worried."

Vince exhaled a lungful of exasperation and released the jerk. He glowered into the man's frightened eyes and demanded, "Do you know what kind of risk your presence poses? What'd they teach you in spy school? Your good intentions could cost Kat her life." Vince uttered another vicious curse.

"She doesn't know. I've been very careful," he protested meekly.

"Yeah, right," Vince growled. "You've been reckless, that's what you've been. I have half a mind to report you to Lucas Camp."

Damrus's eyes rounded. "Oh, I don't want any trouble. I just want to keep an eye on Ms. Moore."

Vince plowed his fingers through his hair. "Then you do it through me. You follow the routine of a professor and never, *ever* tail her again. Do you understand me?"

The man wilted against his car. "Yes. Yes. I'm sorry. I thought I was helping. They wouldn't tell me how she was doing or anything. So—"

"So you tapped into the files and started your own little operation," Vince finished for him. This guy was no operative. He was a research geek. His only field experience had been in the lab.

The man nodded. "I only want to help."

"All right. Maybe you can." Vince scanned the street once more, then thought for a minute. "We need to talk. Where can we meet?" He couldn't risk any more time right now. He didn't like Kat being out of his sight for this long.

Damrus suggested the school library any time tomorrow after two o'clock. He gave Vince his cell phone number, which he committed to memory.

"I'll call you," Vince told him. "Now stay away from this area and Kat except when she's in your class. I'll keep you informed. Count on it."

Damrus nodded and climbed back into his car and drove away. Shaking his head, Vince swung onto his bike and turned around to head the other way. He wasn't surprised to see Callahan waiting in a white SUV at the end of the block. He eased up next to the passenger window, which she immediately powered down.

"I'm not sure I want to know what the hell that was all about," she said pointedly.

"That was Mr. Damrus from the CIA."

Callahan swore. "What's a Company jerk doing here? Trying to blow this operation?"

Vince shook his head. "He's the implant designer. No one knows he's here."

Callahan whistled long and low. "He could have screwed up everything."

"Tell me about it." Vince glanced in the direction he'd last seen Damrus. "He's set himself up a cover at the university as one of the professors."

"I'll have to inform Lucas," Callahan said, giving notice.

"Before you do, I need to talk to this guy a little more. Can you give me twenty-four hours?"

She shrugged. "It's your ass if he blows it."

Vince winked at her. "I'll make sure that doesn't happen."

"You do that," Callahan called behind him as he drove away.

Vince had a lot of questions for Damrus. He needed to make sure Kat was not in danger from the implant.

His gut told him that the headaches and confusion were warnings that things were going very wrong. He'd like to know more right away. But right now he had to get back to the house. He didn't want Kat alone with Yu any more than absolutely necessary.

The house was silent when Vince entered, minutes after his encounter with Damrus. Neither of the SUVs was in the driveway. Jamal had left earlier. Either he had returned and left again with the others, or Kat had. Vince sincerely hoped it was the former. He needed to talk to Kat. He had to know what had happened this morning and led to what he'd walked in on. She didn't owe him an explanation, but he wanted one if she was willing to give it.

He took the stairs two at a time, but slowed and took a deep, calming breath before opening the door and going into their room. He didn't knock.

Kat sat in the middle of the bed studying something on one of Will's laptops. She looked up, her expression immediately going to one of irritation. "Don't even think about starting anything with me," she warned. She shut down the program, then closed the laptop and set it aside.

Vince leaned against the window frame, a safe distance away, and looked at her. "All right. I won't start anything. I won't even ask what happened." He turned his attention to the yard and the street beyond it. If he saw the first sign of that gray sedan he was going to kill Damrus with his bare hands.

He heard the covers rustle, but he didn't look back. Whatever she wanted to tell him, it had to be her decision. His gut clenched again at the thought of her with that—

"You were gone for a long time, Vince," she said softly as she came up beside him, then leaned on the opposite side of the window. "Phil made me laugh... made me forget that I was alone."

Vince suppressed the emotions welling inside him like a tidal wave threatening to drown him. Maybe he didn't want to hear this.

"We hit it off." She sighed and tucked a lock of auburn silk behind her ear. "I needed him."

She looked at Vince then, willing him to look at her. He could feel her insistence. He finally gave in and settled his gaze on her, saw the emotions shining in those emerald depths.

"But it was never anything like what we have," she said quietly. "It was just—"

"Did you…?" He couldn't say it. His jaw hardened, trapping the rest of what he wanted to say.

She shook her head. "It wasn't like that. It wasn't an intimacy we shared on a physical level." She looked away. "Not until today."

"Why?" Vince demanded. "Why did you let him touch you?"

She looked straight at him and denied him what he wanted to hear more than anything else in the world. "I'm not going to try to explain it. It just happened. But it won't happen again."

"If it does—"

"You'll what?" she snapped. "Kill him? Well you'd better watch your back, Ferrelli, because he feels the same way."

She stomped out of the room, slamming the door behind her.

Well, he was batting a thousand today. She'd walked out on him twice.

Vince dropped his head and stared at the carpeted floor. Maybe she was hung up on Yu. Maybe the Romeo option was failing. Just another question he had for Damrus.

He glanced back at the closed door, then at the bed where she'd left the laptop. If nothing else, he could always attempt to do his job. Maybe if she caught him messing with her laptop she'd simply shoot him and put him out of his misery.

Then again maybe he needed to remind her of what they'd once shared. He'd sworn he wouldn't allow things to go that far under the circumstances.

But the circumstances had changed.

THAT NIGHT Kat curled into her pillow, fighting and at the same time surrendering to the dream. Vince was with her. She couldn't make out all the details…everything was fuzzy. But he was there. She felt him.

It was wet…cold. God, so cold.

She had a wool blanket draped around her. He was telling her that she was okay. She's survived yet another evolution. The worst was behind her. Just one more day of "hell week."

It pays to be a winner.

Vince knelt in front of her and chucked her on the chin. "You're a winner, baby." He stood, smiling down at her. He wore military fatigues. As she watched he turned and shouted orders to others sitting around draped in blankets just as she was.

It was so damned cold.

And wet.

The ocean.

In the dream, Kat looked out over the dark, stormy waters.

She had survived the worst.

She looked up.

And Vince was with her.

Kat jerked from the dream.

She struggled to catch her breath. Her skin was slick with sweat. The ocean…the cold…the uniform.

"It's okay, baby," Vince murmured from where he lay next to her in the bed. He reached for her, tried to pull her close. "You're okay."

Kat bolted from the bed, grabbing her weapon from the table as she went.

She was breathing hard. Her fingers clenched around the weapon. Her aim instantly leveled in the direction of the threat.

The bedside lamp came on. She blinked.

Vince squinted at her and then at the gun in her hand. "What's going on?" He pushed the covers back and started to get up. "Did you—"

"Don't move," she warned, her voice low, hoarse. She couldn't trust him. The epiphany came like a revelation from the Almighty, fast and furious. She didn't know what the rest of the dream meant, if anything, but she knew she couldn't trust him.

His expression grew guarded. "It's okay, Kat. You're safe with me. You know me." Something like fear flickered in his eyes, but disappeared so fast she was certain she'd imagined it.

"You're damn straight I know you. You're a liar," she spat. "A liar and a cheat."

He made no attempt to deny her accusations. He just

watched her. Those gray eyes dark with concern. That perfect body, the one she knew by heart, naked save for his briefs. She knew this guy all right.

He was…*Vince.*

And she loved him with all her heart. Her resolve weakened. But she couldn't…

Abruptly a shard of pain splintered in her brain, buckling her knees beneath her.

Just as suddenly Vince had her in his arms. He tossed her weapon aside and held her close. "It's okay," he murmured over and over. "Don't cry."

It wasn't until he said the words that she realized she was crying. The sobs shook her, each one followed by a stab of pain in her skull. What was happening to her?

"I don't know, baby, but we're damn sure going to find out."

Kat clung to him. She must have asked the question out loud. She couldn't think…couldn't tell what was real and what wasn't.

Vince eased down onto the bed, keeping her close until they were both lying amid the thick covers and fluffy pillows.

He kissed her temple. "Go to sleep. I'm right here. Trust me, baby. I'll keep you safe."

Kat snuggled against his chest, allowed the steady beat of his heart to comfort her. She must be losing her mind to believe for one second that Vince would ever do anything to hurt her.

He would never betray her.

Never.

Chapter Nine

"Damrus, we have to talk."

Vince used a pay phone in the parking lot of a gas station while Kat went inside for coffee. He didn't want her to know what he was up to until he had something concrete to offer. He'd worry about persuading her to agree then.

"I told you not to call me until after two," Damrus said in a hushed tone. "I can't leave right now. I'm in the middle of a staff meeting. I—"

"Things have changed," Vince cut him off. "Something happened last night. It can't wait." Every time Vince thought of the way Kat had freaked out last night, he almost panicked. Something was very wrong. Scanning the flow of traffic, he waited impatiently for Damrus to make a decision.

"I'll have to make the arrangements. Where can I call you back?"

Vince saw Kat at the cash register. She'd be coming out soon. "You can't. Give me a time and place."

"I...I have to make calls and—"

"Give me a time and place," Vince demanded, any patience he'd had left a thing of the past.

"One hour. Dr. Alvin Cook's office, 224 Lynwood Avenue."

"You know this guy?" Vince didn't like the idea of involving anyone else. He didn't even like calling Damrus. But he was desperate.

"Yes," Damrus admitted wearily. "I know him. He owes me a favor."

"One hour," Vince reiterated, then hung up.

Kat exited the convenience store and walked toward the Harley. He tried not to focus on the fit of her jeans or the top that allowed an intriguing strip of creamy midriff skin to show. He ached for her on every level.

She frowned when she realized he was walking away from the pay phone. "Something wrong?"

Her instincts were still sharp. Vince accepted the cup of coffee she offered. Now for the hard part. "I've been thinking about last night."

She sipped her coffee and grimaced, more likely from his comment than the brew. "I don't want to think about it." She shivered. "It was too weird."

He leaned against the bike and pulled her between his widespread legs, enjoying the feel of her close to him in such an intimate way. Sleeping with her without making love to her was driving him crazy.

"Look," he began with more understanding than she could imagine, "I know you don't want to think about it, but we need to face this." He laced the fingers of his free hand with hers. "I'm worried about you."

She stared at her cup, avoiding his gaze, but the frown still marred her pretty face. "I'm scared, Vince." She looked at him then. "I don't know what's happening to me." She shook her head slowly. "Everything I'm supposed to know seems all mixed up…some parts lost or so gray I can't see them."

He squeezed her hand. "I made you an appointment with a doctor. We need to get this checked out." She pulled back slightly, her expression skeptical, clearly fearful. He looked deeply into her eyes, willing her to trust him, to see the depth of his concern for her. "Please. Do it for me."

She backed out of the intimate position and tossed her coffee into a trash receptacle. After a hesitation that felt like forever, she met his hopeful gaze. "All right. I'll go, but I don't want Phil or any of the others to know about this."

Vince disposed of his untouched coffee. "Sounds good to me." The less Yu knew, the better Vince liked it.

Kat slid behind him on the bike. If he had his way, he'd leave right now and take Kat as far away from all this as possible. But she'd only end up hating him for blowing the mission.

He resisted the urge to shake his head. As if she wasn't going to hate him anyway.

VINCE WATCHED Dr. Cook's second neurological screening through the open blinds on the window of the examination room. He resisted the urge to pace the corridor yet again. He wanted to be in there with her. She'd been through this once when they'd first arrived. Then a nurse and a technician had put her through a barrage of tests, X rays, CAT scan. Dr. Cook's office wasn't just the average sawbones's office, it was an elaborate neurology clinic.

Dr. Damrus was still reviewing the results of the scan and the X ray.

Vince didn't even want to consider how irate Lucas was going to be when he discovered that Damrus was in the area and that he and Vince had actually hooked up. Vince had screwed up one career, he had no intention of repeating that mistake.

A weary sigh behind him alerted Vince of Damrus's approach. It was a good thing the guy was a scientist, he definitely wasn't cut out for the spy business.

"Give it to me straight, Doc," Vince said, cutting to the chase.

Damrus shrugged and offered his empty palms. "There's nothing to tell. Everything looks fine. There is simply no indication of a developing infection, aneurysm or any other problem around the insertion site."

Aneurysm? "What exactly were you expecting to find?" Vince asked, astonished at the man's cold, clinical attitude.

"I had no way of being certain what I might find, but you can rest assured that all is as it should be."

Vince ground out a curse. "Maybe you had to be there, but I'm telling you that what I witnessed last night was far from fine. She told you about the head-aches, the confusion."

Damrus stared at the woman beyond the glass. "Look, Mr. Ferrelli, this isn't an exact science." He turned to Vince. "She's our first field test of the implant. This is as new to me as it is to you."

Vince silently cursed experimental technology and the CIA, in that order. "That's reassuring."

The older man's brow lined in thought, his attention settling back on Kat. "The most logical conclusion is that she's experiencing breakthrough memories."

"What the hell is that?" Vince felt his tension ratchet up another notch. Whatever Damrus's definition of the term, Vince doubted it would be a good thing.

"The implant is preventing her from accessing stored memory. It acts as a kind of security gate. It blocks the flow of stored memory while offering its own files instead. Much the way a computer can require a password to effectively block access to certain files or programs while leaving others available. Except that the human brain is not precisely like a simple computer." He sighed again. "Kat's mind may be working overtime to bypass the implant. Thus, breakthrough memories."

Definitely not a good thing.

"What do we do about that?" Neither he nor Kat would be safe if her memory downloaded at the wrong time and place, which at the moment, was most anytime or anywhere.

Damrus shook his head slowly from side to side. "I don't know."

Vince couldn't believe his ears. "You don't know?" he echoed, then snapped back control and lowered his voice. "You designed this thing and you don't know?"

"Unfortunately not. If we suggest information to her to bait her mind in hopes of pinpointing possible break-throughs, we could confuse her further. So we can't judge if there has already been any significant corruption to the implant's function. Our best course of action is to carry on and see what happens. We don't want any more of her real past getting scrambled with the assumed past."

"Worst case scenario," Vince pressed. "I want to know what's the worst I can expect and how to handle it."

Damrus looked at him frankly. "The worst…" He swallowed with effort. "Since we see no risk of aneurysm or unnecessary clotting, the worst that could happen would be a psychotic episode."

Vince's eyes bulged. He went as cold as ice. "Is any of this going to do permanent damage?"

Damrus shook his head adamantly. "No. No. I'm sure of that much. Any permanent damage would have already been apparent. What we need to concern our-selves with now is mental stability."

Vince looked at Kat through the aluminum slats of the blind. He wanted that damned implant out of her—*now.* But he knew that wasn't going to happen. "So what do I do…if the worst case scenario happens?"

Damrus handed Vince a small packet containing three pills. "This will help. If she suffers an episode like last night's again, give her one of these pills. It should calm her down very quickly."

"What is it?" Vince studied the pills but didn't recognize them as anything he'd ever seen before.

"Anti-psychotics." Damrus leveled his gaze on Vince. "Don't give her the medication unless there is no other option. It could pose its own problems."

Vince looked at the pills again and then at the doctor.

"This—" Damrus nodded to the packet in Vince's hand "—must be a last resort." Then he disappeared to avoid being noticed by Kat, leaving Vince with even more questions than before.

SHE WAS FINE.

Kat felt as if a weight had been lifted from her chest. Dr. Cook had assured her that her headaches and confusion were brought on by stress, nothing more. Lots of students who held down full-time jobs in addition to their studies, suffered with stress and anxiety-related problems.

If the man only knew what her job was.

Kat almost laughed.

She felt one hundred percent better.

She looked at Vince as he swung off the Harley. God, she loved to look at him. All fluid movement and grace. He'd been really worried about her. It touched her deeply that he'd insisted she see a doctor.

"Looks like the gang's all here," Vince said, dragging her from the admiration session that was making her hot and bothered.

It was time she showed him just how much she cared. Things had been a little rocky the past couple of days. They needed to put that behind them now. Kiss and make up. A wicked grin lifted the corners of her mouth. And tonight would be the perfect time. Jamal, Leva and Will always hit the bars on Friday nights. Didn't even make it home most of the time. Phil had a face-to-face with The Man; he'd told her this morning. A twinge of guilt tweaked her at that thought. Phil had insisted she not tell Vince about his meeting. She didn't like keeping things from him. She pushed it away. No more. She wasn't going to worry about anything else today…or *tonight*.

"Earth to Kat."

Kat jerked her attention back to the present. "I'm sorry, I zoned out for a moment."

Vince smiled, one of those true Ferrelli charmers. "I'd love to know where you went. Judging by that wicked grin on your face, I'd like to go there with you."

She winked at him and sauntered toward the house. "Don't worry, you will."

Vince opened the door for Kat, then followed her into the house. The rest of the team was gathered around the dining table in deep discussion. Four sets of eyes shot up when the door slammed.

A strategy meeting. And he and Kat hadn't been invited.

"Kat, we waited for you," Phil said, smiling at her as if his words were entirely genuine. But she knew better.

Vince muttered something rude under his breath.

"I can see that." Kat's tone was sharp, slightly accusing. "What'd I miss?"

"We're finished here for now," Phil said, glancing from Kat to Vince and back. "I'll bring you up to speed…later." He looked Vince's way once more when he said the last.

"Well, I've got places to go and people to see," Will announced abruptly. He gathered his papers and laptop and made short work of the stairs.

"See ya'll in the morning," Jamal said, taking his cue from Will. "I got a date."

Kat didn't like this one little bit. In fact, if her temper continued on its present course, she would reach the boiling point in about five seconds.

"What the hell is this, Phil?"

Leva pushed up and swaggered past Kat, tossing her a look as she went. "Come with me, Ferrelli. I've got some things to show you in my shop."

Vince made no move to follow her, his attention focused on Phil. Kat had a feeling he had no intention of leaving her alone with Phil again.

"She's right," Kat said icily. "You should let Leva familiarize you with her newest design. It's the one we'll be using for the main event." She wanted to have a few words with Phil. *Alone.*

Vince still didn't look happy about it. He sent Phil a warning look, then followed Leva downstairs.

"What's going on?" Kat moved to the table where Phil still stood. "Did you purposely leave me out of this briefing?"

He pulled a chair out next to where he stood. "I didn't schedule it."

That could only mean that The Man had. Kat's pulse rate kicked up. She sat in the offered chair. "Have there been any changes?"

156   *Her Hidden Truth*

"Only one or two." Phil took the chair next to hers. "Nothing we can't handle."

Being alone with him again after what happened yesterday made Kat nervous. She didn't want to have to reject him outright, but if he continued to push the issue she'd have no choice.

"Why are you keeping Vince in the dark?" she asked, turning the conversation to something besides her.

Phil draped an arm around the back of her chair. "He doesn't need to know the final details just yet." His gaze connected fully with hers. "If you break protocol, you will endanger his life as well as your own."

"I understand."

He would kill Vince if Kat interfered. She didn't question it. She knew he would. Phil wanted her...saw Vince as an obstacle. But Phil was also a man of his word. All he needed, however, was one little excuse to consider himself absolved of that responsibility and that would be that.

Phil leaned closer, putting his head next to hers as they studied the schematics on his laptop. "This will be our defining moment, Kat." He looked at her, his face only centimeters from her cheek. "Once we have accomplished this mission, we will have achieved the highest status WSA has to offer. We will have made our place and honored this country with our selflessness."

Kat told herself he was right. She'd watched the news and from all reports, ICS had pledged to come back with an impenetrable system. A way of maintaining unbreachable security for its clients. The efforts of this team had forced a complacent company who had long ago monopolized the security industry to reach for higher standards and to take notice of the changing world it promised to keep safe.

This team, as many others around the globe belonging to WSA, represented the silent warriors who risked their lives to make the world a better place.

Why didn't she feel the anticipation and pride she once had? She focused on the screen in front of her in the hope that Phil would not read her conflicting emotions. Nothing felt right anymore. She stared at the screen.

Taking his time, he slowly turned his attention to the monitor and away from her. Kat suppressed the need to exhale her relief. She and Phil were on the same side. She had to remember that.

Somehow she kept forgetting.

LEVA'S SHOP.

It was a pretty impressive little setup. Vince wasn't really surprised to see it. After all, all bomb freaks had them. He was surprised by her supply of goods. Mostly military-grade explosives, she had enough "boom" ingredients, mixes and associated additives, detonators, etcetera, to blow the whole city off the map. The Alcohol, Tobacco and Firearms folks were going to have a field day with this.

Sleeping only two floors above this growing stockpile gave him absolutely no comfort.

Leva's new design was nothing short of elegant. Not your fly-by-night concoction of pipes and loads, but a sophisticated layout of wires, detonators and explosives all in a sweet black case. Every single item was meticulously constructed, for function as well as presentation. There would be a total of four explosions. The primary, a blast no one in a five-block radius would forget, and then a series of three small secondary detonations in strategic locations.

This was meant to take out more than a simple building. Vince wished like hell he knew the target. But no amount of charm had pried the information from Leva. Even his quick look at the files on Kat's laptop had yielded nothing. The one file he thought might contain what he needed was blocked, requiring a password. One he hadn't had time to try to decode.

"So, Ferrelli." Leva sidled up to him. "What do you think?"

"I think you're a crackerjack boomer," he said with all the charm he could inflect.

She traced the row of buttons down the front of his shirt. "I could be a lot more, if you'd only let me."

Vince took her hand in his, held it a moment, then moved it safely away from him, resisting a shudder of revulsion. "I couldn't do that to Kat."

She inclined her head. "Why not? She and Philip certainly share something the rest of us don't."

Vince tamped down the jealous rage that rose instantly whenever Kat's and Yu's names were uttered in the same sentence. He knew this jealousy was dangerous to both of them, but he just couldn't help it.

"If we're all done here, I have other things to do." He

hadn't meant to allow the edge in this tone, but it had been there all the same. "Thanks for the nickel tour," he called over his shoulder as he headed for the stairs. Yu had been alone with Kat too long.

Vince told himself that his sudden urge to get upstairs had nothing to do with what Leva said…but he knew better. She'd reminded him of what he already feared. Damrus had admitted he couldn't say what to expect from the implant. It might cause Kat to do things she wouldn't normally do. She no longer knew she was a CIA operative under deep cover. She didn't know that she was working for the enemy at the moment. She sure as hell didn't know it was his job to salvage this mission and to make sure her new friends failed.

Vince slowed as he came to the end of the hallway where it merged with the living room. He watched for one long moment. Kat smiled at Yu. He pointed to something on the screen, leaning as close as possible in doing so. His arm was around the back of her chair. This was what Yu wanted. To have Kat all to himself. Vince wondered if Yu would still have involved her if he'd known that, more likely than not, the whole team would die as soon as their mission was completed.

Yu was the one and only exception to WSA's consistent record of tying up all loose ends. In Vince's opinion, that was too bad for Yu and his pals. If Yu had died like the others, he wouldn't be here now trying to charm Kat. But then, that was Vince's jealousy speaking. Human life was far more important than petty jealousy.

It just didn't feel that way at the moment.

But he had to remember that Will, Jamal, Leva and even Yu thought they were the good guys.

Vince cleared his throat and walked into the room, straight up to the table. He sat next to Kat. Yu immediately closed the laptop.

"Can I help you, Ferrelli?"

Vince bent forward and kissed Kat's cheek just to tick off Yu. "Absolutely," he said in answer to the question. The guy was glowering at him now. "You can bring me up to speed. If I'm in, I shouldn't be kept in the dark."

Before Yu could answer, Leva strutted through the room. "I'm going out. Be back later."

Kat glanced at Leva then at Vince, the "What happened?" question written all over her face.

Vince would talk to her when they were alone. Right now he had to try to provoke Yu into coming clean with him. Seducing it from Kat was a last resort. He couldn't afford to do anything that would jeopardize her tenuous stability.

"Am I in or out?" Vince pressed.

Kat pushed back her chair and got up. "I think I'll call for a pizza. Anyone hungry?"

Yu ignored her, so did Vince. Their gazes were locked in silent communication…silent battle. Both of them wanted the same thing—to take this to the mat.

"I know a place," Yu said, reading Vince's mind. "It's nearby."

"Let's do it," Vince suggested, his heart rate already climbing in anticipation.

"What's going on?" Kat looked from one to the other, suspicious. "I don't like the sound of this."

Yu turned a stern look in her direction. "We have business to attend to. We'll be back."

She shook her head. "No. Wait. This is completely—"

Vince held up a restraining hand when she would have argued further. "We have to settle this." He tossed a confident look at his opponent. "We'll be back in an hour—tops."

He regretted the look of sheer helplessness on her face as she watched them go.

But this was the only way.

Vince and his nemesis had to settle their differences once and for all.

If Yu wouldn't trust him, Vince had to at least earn his respect.

Since he wasn't a vital part of the team, this was the only way. And he would win.

Vince could take anyone to the mat.

Chapter Ten

Like every other college town in America, by dark on a Friday night, most of the temporary residents were hanging out at some bar, club or urban-style restaurant. The dateless and those with a cash-flow problem crashed at one of the numerous frat houses, unless a guy was all of the above and liked to pump iron.

The four young men who had chosen to do the latter, immediately stopped what they were doing, grabbed their stuff and departed from the premises when Philip Yu entered the low-rent private gym on Center Street. Apparently Yu had developed himself quite a reputation around town during the six months he'd lived here.

Bob's Gym wasn't very large, but would suffice. Middle-of-the-line weight benches and not much else lined the walls. There were a couple of doors leading toward the back of the building. Rest rooms and an office, Vince guessed.

Yu stripped off his watch and belt, then his sneakers. Vince didn't feel the need to preface his performance with any kind of ritual that served as nothing more than a clichéd intimidation tactic.

Vince was not intimidated. They'd locked their weapons in the SUV as a show of sportsmanship. They were on even ground.

"We have a problem, *friend*," Yu said. He braced his hands at his waist and moved to the center of the large matted area.

Vince met him halfway. "Now there's something we can agree on." He shrugged. "The way I see it, that's about all we have in common, *friend*."

Yu's expression darkened. "I gave Kat my word that you could remain a part of our team." He began to circle Vince slowly, his gaze never deviating from its target. "That I can deal with until you give me reason not to. However, the rest of the team recognizes your lack of respect for me and I will not tolerate that."

"So this is about respect?" Vince suggested, his tone making clear his doubt. He clocked Yu's movements, recognizing his strategy for what it was—a distraction.

"In part," Yu replied frankly. "I will have your respect if you are to continue as a member of this team. I will have the woman you claim…either way."

Vince only smiled. "You'll have to kill me first," he warned.

An answering smile slid across Yu's face. "That could be arranged, but won't be necessary."

Gut check. An alarm went off in Vince's head. He stilled, studying his opponent's posture, his tone. Yu had something up his sleeve. Vince had the overwhelming urge to look behind him, but he refused to take his gaze off Yu.

"You won't take her from me," Vince told him flatly. "Not in this lifetime."

"That is yet to be seen." The man's confidence went over and above assurance and into the territory of arrogance. "Enough talk."

"Something else we can agree on," Vince allowed, his anticipation surging. He wanted to take this guy down in the worst way.

Then everything changed.

Beyond Yu, in the long mirror weight lifters used to study their form, Vince caught a glimpse of reflected movement behind him. At that same instant Yu made his move.

ARMS FOLDED in annoyance over her chest, Kat stared at the nappy carpet just to make sure she hadn't paced a hole in it. More than an hour had passed and Vince wasn't back yet. She hadn't seen Phil, either. The pizza she'd ordered was cold and unopened. She walked to the window again and peered out into the night.

Nothing.

She massaged her throbbing temple. Damn, she wished the headache would go away. She'd taken too much aspirin already. Maybe she should have asked Dr. Cook for something stronger. The over-the-counter stuff was useless.

The telephone rang and Kat froze.

What if it was the police?

What if Vince was hurt really badly…and—

The telephone rang again.

Kat dismissed the ridiculous notion. Vince could hold his own with Phil. No question.

She picked up the receiver on the third ring. "Hello?"

"Kat, this is Will."

She heard loud music in the background. She smiled, thinking he was probably at his favorite hangout. The thought made her frown. Why didn't she have a favorite place to go? Maybe she did and she'd simply forgotten about it. A stab of pain punctuated the sad realization. She massaged the back of her head and forced the silly notions away. Her fingers stilled, then moved more slowly. For the first time she noticed a small hard ridge in her flesh. Then again, maybe she'd simply forgotten it was there. She traced the line that was no more than an inch in length and racked her brain to recall its origin. Nothing came.

Forcing her attention back to the phone, she asked, "What's up, Will? You need a designated driver already?" It wasn't that late, surely he wasn't soused this early.

"Look," he said, his tone suddenly uncharacteristically serious. "Phil would kill me for telling you this, but I just can't…"

"What is it?" Fear snaked around Kat's heart. Her mind emptied of all else. "Does this have something to do with Vince?"

Will hesitated, sighed. "Yeah." Another gut-wrenching pause. Music blared in the background. "Phil wants to teach Vince a lesson in humility. They planned the whole thing while you guys were out today. And, uh, just in case he can't take him alone, he's got J-Man waiting in the wings. They're gonna work him over good."

The grip of fear tightened. "Where are they?" They hadn't told her where they were going. She had no idea where to begin looking. She glanced at the clock and swore. They'd already been gone plenty long enough to do the job. No matter where they were, she wouldn't get there in time to stop Phil.

"Bob's Gym over on Center. You can't tell 'em I told you, Kat. Do you hear me?"

"I won't. I gotta go, Will."

"Yeah, okay." He hung up.

Kat dropped the phone, raced up the stairs and slung clothes and books aside until she located the extra set of keys Vince had given her to the Harley. She shoved her weapon into her jeans and lunged down the stairs, almost falling in her haste.

She should have known Phil would play dirty. He intended to get Vince one way or another. Anger boiled up inside her, almost overtaking the fear. Phil would answer to her on this one. The power trip he'd been on lately was over. It wasn't supposed to be this way. They were equals. It was his job to organize and lead, not bully and threaten.

The fifteen minutes it took to get to the gym felt like as many hours. She barreled into the parking lot, skidding to a stop right in front of the double doors and parked the bike. The SUV was not in sight.

God, she was too late.

She jerked open the door and rushed inside.

Silence greeted her.

The place looked and sounded empty.

Her heart surged into her throat and seemed to stop beating right there. She couldn't breathe. Tears burned in her eyes. She wanted to call out his name, but couldn't manage the effort. She stood in the middle of the big, deserted room and sagged with defeat.

She was too late.

A sound echoed from behind a closed door. Kat listened intently as she eased toward the door on the right. The continued silence almost convinced her that she'd only been hearing things. Wishful thinking that Vince might still be here.

Then she heard it.

Running water.

Hope propelled her heart back into action. She ran the remaining steps to the door, then stopped. Forcing herself to take a breath, she opened the door as quietly as possible. She knew better than to walk through a door without checking things out first.

A shower room. The smell of mold and mildew hit her nostrils. One second later her eyes found what she was looking for…what she prayed she would find.

Thank God.

He was alive.

Vince stood at one of the sinks, a wad of wet paper towels in his hand. Too weak with relief to move or to speak, her gaze followed as he lifted his hand to his face.

Blood. Lots of blood.

Kat gasped.

Vince wheeled in her direction.

Fury seared away her fear, she stormed across the dingy tile floor and pulled Vince's hand away to get a closer look. She cursed Phil at length.

"My sentiments exactly," Vince said dryly, then winced when she touched his forehead.

Kat surveyed the damage more thoroughly, trying her best not to think about the fact that this face belonged to Vince. The corner of his lip was busted. His left cheek was swollen just like the last time he'd been in a brawl. The eye would be black this time. She sighed. The big problem was the damage right above his left eyebrow. She was pretty sure that was going to require professional medical attention for closure. She shook her head in abject disgust and cursed Phil again.

Focusing on what had to be done, she folded several paper towels and pressed the makeshift bandage to the wound. Vince's jaw hardened and he blinked rapidly. Must hurt like hell, she imagined.

"Hold this," she instructed.

He obeyed.

She wet another handful of towels and scrubbed the blood from the side of his face as best she could. She tossed the bloodied towels into the trash and ushered him toward the door. "Let's go someplace where I can patch you up and think this through."

There was a pharmacy on Main that kept later hours than most. Hopefully the place would still be open. She'd pick up a few things and see what she could do.

Kat glanced at Vince and felt her knees weaken. He moved stiffly and was far too quiet. He'd taken a bad beating. There could be other injuries that weren't obvious just yet. She watched him closely as he mounted the bike. He winced sharply and clutched his abdomen. She swore again. There were too many frightening possibilities to name.

"Don't even think about it," Vince growled. "You take me straight to the house. I want to finish this business with Yu." Fury glinted in those steel-gray eyes. "Just the two of us this time."

He'd known she was considering the hospital emergency room. Kat climbed on in front of him. "Not tonight, big boy."

"I mean it, Kat." He placed a hand on her arm when she would have started the engine. "I'm finishing this tonight."

The feral sound of his voice made her shiver, as much with desire as with fear that he meant exactly what he said. He was in no condition to square things with Phil tonight.

There was only one way she knew of to keep him from following through with his determined vow.

A distraction.

And this one had been a long time in coming.

VINCE MOPPED HIS BODY dry with a clean towel. Kat had insisted he shower while she went for first-aid supplies. She'd also insisted they needed some time away from Yu and the others. Vince had started to argue, but then she'd kissed him. His hands slowed in their work of drying. Not just any kiss. One that promised more to come.

A lot more.

His body reacted even now.

He hadn't been able to say no.

So they'd checked into a cheap motel on the outskirts of Port Charlotte.

Gingerly running the towel over his hair, Vince contemplated the nasty wound on his forehead. The bleeding had slowed, but Kat was right: a few stitches or staples were probably in order. Vince had been surprised that Will had given Kat a heads-up.

Vince gritted his teeth at the thought of Yu's treachery. Callahan had freaked out when she'd found Vince on the floor of the gym. She'd made her way to the back of the building when she'd seen Jamal doing the same. She'd followed him inside without his ever knowing she was shadowing him. She'd hated like hell to stand by and watch the two-against-one fight. But stepping in hadn't been an option as long as Vince appeared to be holding his own. The final blow Jamal had wielded with the weight bar had almost brought her out of her hiding place. But Yu had told Jamal that it was enough…for now. The two men had left and Callahan had rushed to Vince's aid.

As soon as she'd helped him to the nearest water supply to clean up the blood, Vince had insisted that she get lost. He could take care of himself. No point risking anyone finding her there with him. Callahan hadn't wanted to leave but she'd known it was the right thing to do.

As soon as she was out the door, Vince had slid down the wall to the floor and just sat there, struggling to keep from blacking out.

He pressed a hand to his side. Judging by the pain level, he'd wager he had a fractured rib or two. No way was he telling Callahan or Kat. He wasn't going to a hospital. He could live with this. He'd lived with worse.

By the time Kat had found him, he'd managed to drag himself back to his feet and had started to clean up the blood.

Vince wrapped a towel around his waist, every move a test of endurance. Palming his weapon, it hit him just how tired he was.

Then he remembered that kiss he and Kat had shared before she'd left and the promise it held.

He might be banged up and tired as hell, but he wasn't dead.

Since Kat wasn't back yet, Vince allowed the towel to drop. He tucked his weapon under his pillow and climbed naked between the cool sheets. He clenched his jaw against the pain that accompanied his movements. Closing his eyes, he surrendered to the weariness. When Kat returned he'd be ready for whatever she had in mind.

A small smile twitched at the undamaged corner of his mouth. Being with Kat again would be worth whatever discomfort it cost him.

KAT STORED THE ITEMS she would need to patch up Vince beneath the seat of the Harley. Her rage had grown to a level where she could hardly think around it. She swung onto the bike and started the engine. It wasn't until she'd gotten up to the register to pay that she noticed the dried blood on her right arm. Vince's blood. Any ability to reason had left her at that point.

Phil had allowed personal feelings to influence his conduct as team leader. That was a bigger mistake than even he knew. Kat had every intention of calling it to his attention. And making sure it didn't happen again. She knew just how to handle that problem, as well.

She'd teach him a lesson he wouldn't soon forget.

The room was dark when she arrived. He was sleeping soundly. Kat smiled knowingly as she stripped off her clothes and toed off her sneakers right next to the door. As she silently approached the bed she wore only two things, her panties and her weapon strapped to her ankle. She smiled again. He would appreciate that.

Her eyes had adjusted to the darkness, allowing her to make out his form against the white sheets. She climbed onto the foot of the bed, moving stealthily on all fours like a panther about to pounce on its prey.

He jerked awake.

"It's me," she murmured, infusing a sensual sultriness into her tone.

He relaxed into the pillows, flat on his back now, waiting, anticipating her next move.

She didn't disappoint him. She moved up his long legs, straddling him, allowing the length of her hair to drag along the thin sheet. The change in his breathing was audible, but he didn't speak...afraid of breaking the spell.

When her torso was even with his, her knees on either

side of his waist, she leaned in close to his face, her lips mere centimeters from his. "Is this what you want?"

He pulled her to him, kissed her hard. She didn't resist.

She brushed intimately against his fully aroused loins, her calves clenched at his sides. He groaned savagely and kissed her even harder.

She had the gun in her hand and pressed against his male equipment before his lust-encumbered brain could register the movement. She'd teach him to put his personal feelings before the good of the team.

Phil's head dropped back, his breath ragged against her face. "What the hell are you doing?" he demanded.

"You've been thinking with your little friend here instead of your brain, Philip," she accused. She kept her face close to his, her breasts just touching his bare chest, the tip of the barrel firm against the base of his erection. "It's a bad thing. I don't like this power trip you're on. I liked you the way you were before." She moved closer to his mouth, tempting him yet again. His breath caught. "What happened to that guy? He was a good leader…a good friend."

"You're angry because—"

"Yes," she cut him off. "How do you think The Man would feel about your little antics? This is supposed to be about something bigger than us. We aren't supposed to take unnecessary risks or to call attention to our-selves. Have you forgotten why we're here?"

She knew that would hit home.

He tensed on a different level. "How could I?"

"Then stop acting like a jealous ass and start acting

like the man, the leader I was drawn to. I wouldn't be here if it wasn't for you, Phil. Don't make me regret it."

She started to back away; he stopped her with a hand on her neck. She tensed automatically, but his touch wasn't threatening, it was gentle…his voice heavy with remorse when he spoke.

"I didn't do this to hurt you. He doesn't deserve you," he said harshly.

Kat pulled away from his touch. "That's not your call to make."

She stood and moved back to the door for her clothes.

"And if he's a traitor?" Phil asked. He made no move to follow her or to stop her or even to turn on the light.

"Then I'll kill him myself." She tugged on her jeans, then her T-shirt.

"You're going to him now?" His words were cold, emotionless.

"Yes." She pushed her feet back into her sneakers without untying them.

"You have that much faith in him?" Another unnervingly cold question.

"Yes."

"I'll be waiting."

Kat left, Phil's final words echoing in her ears. He hadn't meant he'd be waiting for her return to the house. He'd meant that he'd be waiting when she had to admit that he was right. He was that sure Vince was a traitor.

Vince was not a traitor.

She knew it with all her heart.

She closed the front door behind her and double-timed it down to where she'd left the bike at the end of the block. She'd known Phil would hear her coming if she drove into the driveway.

She straddled the leather seat and turned the key. The engine roared to life, drowning out the accusation still ringing in her ears.

Vince was not a traitor. She knew him.

She just couldn't remember certain things about their past together.

Banishing the doubt, she pointed the Harley in the direction of the hotel. She wanted to be alone with Vince tonight. To make long, slow love with him.

To shake loose some of those memories that would reinforce what she already knew.

Vince was not a traitor.

He would never betray her.

Chapter Eleven

Vince roused at the sound of the key turning in the lock of the motel door. He opened his eyes to darkness as well as enough pain to make him groan out loud.

He reached beneath his pillow and snagged his weapon. The light on the bedside table clicked on. He blinked, his weapon leveled toward the intrusion.

"You're not going to need that, Ferrelli," Kat said. She peered down at him, concern marring her expression. "You look like hell."

"Feel like it, too," he muttered as he tucked his weapon away. He glanced at the white bag she held. "I hope that's dinner."

She nodded toward the table near the door. "No, that's dinner. This is torture in a bag."

He pushed himself up into a sitting position and pain stabbed through his side. A breath hissed between his clenched teeth. "Aspirin?" He looked up at her worried eyes and feigned a smile.

She propped both pillows behind him and eased

him back against them. "Be still and shut up, Ferrelli," she ordered.

He wasn't going to argue with that.

She disappeared into the tiny bathroom, then came back with a glass of water and two pills. He swallowed them and drank the water without question.

She sat on the edge of the bed and studied him once more. "This isn't going to be fun." She touched his forehead with gentle fingers.

"I can handle it," he assured her. If she had remembered the night after that trainee went schizoid on him, she'd know he'd been through worse. He looked away. But that past was not a part of this present. He had to remember that.

He couldn't take advantage of the fact that she didn't.

"I said be still," she scolded.

Vince gritted his teeth for the next few minutes as she cleaned the wound over his eye, applied antibiotic ointment, taped the sides together with butterfly strips and covered it with a bandage. As she said, it wasn't fun. But he'd learned a long time ago to compartmentalize the misery.

"Okay." She put the remaining supplies back in the bag. "Stand up."

He tensed, then laughed a choked sound. "I can't."

She frowned. "Are you injured that badly?"

He wagged his head. "I just, uh, I'm naked."

A muscle contracted in his jaw. Could he have sounded any more lame?

Puzzled, she said, "So?"

When he still didn't move, she went on, "It's not like I haven't seen you naked plenty of times before."

Just not in the past four years. "Well, yeah, but…" He gestured vaguely to the lamp. "With the light on and—"

"Fine." She started to turn away, then suddenly she yanked the sheet clean off him. "Now that I've uncovered the mystery, *stand up.*"

Vince froze when her gaze locked on his lower anatomy.

She stared appreciatively at his aroused state. Dammit. That had been the problem. Despite the pain, her every touch had sent desire pumping through his veins, hardening every muscle in his body…some more than others.

Kat waited, hands on hips, for him to obey her order. Gritting his teeth once more against the pain he knew would come, he swung his legs over the side of the bed and stood.

He closed his eyes and focused on denying the pain, on regaining his balance.

She touched his arm. He flinched at the heat generated by just that touch.

"Steady there," she murmured.

She walked him out a few feet from the bed. "Now, hold your arms away from your sides for me."

He did as she instructed. Under other circumstances this granite-like condition might have been nice…but this was definitely not the right situation.

"Wow," she said breathlessly, her attention once more riveted to the appendage with the mind of its own.

"Can you tell me why I'm standing like this?" he demanded, annoyed that he was embarrassed, embarrassed that he *felt* naked in front of Kat. Where was his confidence? They had shared the deepest level of intimacy humanly possible…at one time.

She sighed dreamily, then reached back into the bag and withdrew two large rolls of Ace bandages.

He scowled. "What the hell is that for?"

She gave him a pointed look. "I saw you grab your abdomen earlier. And I've been watching the way you move. I'm not stupid, Vince. You've probably got a cracked rib or two. What the hell did he hit you with, anyway?" As she spoke her fingers peeled away the plastic wrap around the bandage.

"One of the weight bars," he answered. "I was distracted by Yu and didn't see it coming."

Kat hissed a curse. "That won't happen again."

He didn't bother analyzing her statement. She couldn't know that Yu wouldn't try again. When he would have pursued the issue, those skilled fingers dragged across his skin. He forgot the question. She walked around him, unfurling the bandage and pressing it against his skin. Her fingers felt soft and cool. She reached and stretched, her arms brushing his flesh…her body almost touching his…her hip pressed against him. Vince groaned.

"You shouldn't do that," he warned.

She tightened the bandage; he groaned again. This time it had nothing to do with pleasure and everything to do with a spear of pain.

"Why not?" She stepped in closer, making the final

adjustments. The denim of her jeans brushed his hardened flesh.

"Kat," he murmured. "You're driving me crazy."

She smiled. "That was the point." She looked down between them and surveyed his throbbing erection, then back up at him. "Don't you guys do that to virgins?" She arched an auburn eyebrow in question. "You kiss them, nibble their earlobes, and all that other stuff and then you deflower them in one fell swoop."

Vince laughed, his side ached in echo. "Well, I suppose that's true."

"Damn right it is." She looped her arms around his neck and leaned into his chest. He closed his eyes with the pleasure-pain. She tiptoed and whispered in his ear. "Get back into bed, Ferrelli. I've got plans for you."

He took her by the arms and set her just slightly away. "Kat, I—"

"Have run out of excuses," she finished for him. "Bed." She pointed to the tangled sheets.

Vince swallowed hard. He shouldn't do this…she would only hate him all the more in the end. Kat peeled off her T-shirt, revealing her unrestrained breasts. His mouth went dry with want.

"Relax, Vince," she told him, those eyes playing havoc with his ability to think clearly. "I'm going to take care of everything."

Any valid reason not to do this evaporated when she toed off her shoes and wiggled out of those well-fitting jeans. Oblivious to the pain, he settled onto the middle of the bed and watched as she unstrapped her concealed weapon and tossed it aside. His heart hammered in anticipation. Four years…would she remember him… really remember him when they made love?

She dragged her panties along her thighs, taking her time, making it so damned erotic he could hardly bear it. All that silky red hair fell around her shoulders when she straightened. He longed to touch it…to touch her.

She climbed onto the bed, moving up beside him on all fours. She kissed his lips, softly, slowly until he thought he would go mad with it. He touched her hair, tangled his fingers in those silken tresses, his body shuddering at the knowledge that right now, at this moment, she was his in every sense of the word.

His hands roamed over her…sweet, sweet, familiar territory. Feminine swells and valleys, warm and smooth, lean but soft. All woman. His palms traced the gentle contour of her spine, the faint ridges of her rib cage, then the perfect, firm globes of her breasts. The feel of her hands on him was just as he remembered it. Her touch was etched into his mind, tattooed on his heart. Something he could never forget.

She kissed her way down his body, over the bandage, then down to his pulsing sex. She nuzzled him intimately, took him to the brink with that lush, lush mouth. He watched her moving over him, his heart bursting with something he couldn't name. She moved away, leaving him on the verge of climax. He groaned, brutally squashing the need to roll her over, thrust deep inside her and come with all the force that had been building inside him the past few days—few years.

Her sweet torture didn't stop. She'd taken him so close...and now she was killing him with soft little kisses all along his skin. He closed his eyes and struggled to regain some semblance of control.

She kissed her way back up to his mouth, traced the seam of his lips. He opened, but instead of kissing him, she offered him her breast. He sucked deeply, pleasure cascading through him. She hovered over him on all fours, not allowing her slight weight to rest on his battered body. His hand went to the other breast. He massaged, tugged, and then turned to give it equal attention with his mouth. Her breathing was ragged, just like his own.

"I can't wait any longer," she whispered, her words desperate, thick with need.

"Wait." He grasped her waist, stalling the move she intended. He slipped his hand between her thighs and tested her readiness. Her feminine skin was petal-smooth, the nest of curls there downy-soft, the valley beyond as hot as sin. Any hold he still had on sanity vanished.

He eased her hips downward. She guided him. They both cried out when his tip nudged that hot wetness. Slowly, so very slowly, she sank onto him, sheathing him like a velvet glove. She closed her eyes and threw her head back. Vince arched his hips, sinking even more deeply into her, growling like a wild animal.

Neither of them moved for one long beat.

It was too perfect, too delicious. In that moment Vince knew what it was that had welled in his chest moments ago. He had known this level of desire, this level of need, only with her. Realization sent a sweet ache rushing through him as if it had only been days since they'd last made love, not years.

When she opened her eyes and looked into his, he saw the hint of desperation, the intensity of the pleasure they had known only with each other. She felt it, too. And then she began to move. All thought ceased.

His fingers fisted in the sheet, his hips rose to meet her every undulation. She was as tight as a fist and as hot as Hades. Faster, harder, she rode him until she arched her spine and cried out his name.

He couldn't take it anymore. Vince pulled her to him, rolled until she was beneath him and thrust deeply. She cried out again, her inner muscles clenching him, dragging him to the brink once more. He found her mouth, kissed her until she wilted, until the tension seeped from her body, then he began the slow in-and-out movements again.

Slowly. In and out. First only an inch or two…then more…deeper…just a little faster. She clutched his shoulders. Begged him to hurry, but he refused. He gritted his teeth and focused on taking her beyond that ultimate peak once more.

He braced his weight on one arm, tucked the other beneath her and pulled her against him. He wanted her tight little breasts and rock-hard little nipples creating that incredible friction against his bare skin above the bandage. He pumped harder, sweat forming on his brow. He couldn't stop the spiral this time. She arched like a bow, sealing her hips against him, her second climax coming even harder than the first, and then he fell over the edge…his release involving every part of him to the farthest reaches of his soul.

She was his.

For now.

KAT AWOKE with a jolt just before dawn. She'd been dreaming again. Only this time she remembered nothing. Vince slept like the dead next to her. She slipped out of his arms and went to the bathroom.

After using the toilet she ducked her head under the faucet and drank long and deep. Her throat was dry from panting and crying out Vince's name. She smiled, reveled in the afterglow of their lovemaking. She fussed with her hair, studying her tousled yet satisfied reflection.

She thought about the way she'd suffered a moment of déjà vu when she was wrapping that bandage around Vince's torso. He'd been hurt like that before…she couldn't remember exactly when, but she knew he had. She'd played doctor that time, too. And like this time, they'd made love. She reached back and touched the small ridge or scar on the back of her scalp. A frown tugged at her. She should know about that.

A blinding flash of light pierced her skull, the pain accompanying it buckled her knees. Kat sank to the floor. She scrambled to the toilet and heaved until she lost her breath. She flushed the toilet and crawled back to the sink, barely possessing the strength to pull herself up to rinse her mouth before collapsing back onto the floor.

Her eyes closed tightly, she sagged against the wall

and waited to recover from the shakes now racking her weak body.

What was happening to her?

She tried to call out for Vince, but couldn't form the words.

Helpless, she remained slumped there as flash after flash of her life strobed through her brain like film through a runaway projector. None of it made sense. Yet she somehow knew it was all true. Fear bloomed inside her, expanding so fast that she lost her breath.

This couldn't be right.

She knew who she was.

Didn't she?

Dread pooled in her already quivering stomach.

A realization slowly settled amid the chaos in her reeling mind. She was not who she thought she was. That one hidden truth was suddenly perfectly, inexplicably clear.

But who, exactly, was she?

Somehow Vince was involved.

He knew.

Long minutes, maybe hours, passed before Kat could move. Finally she crawled to the shower and climbed inside. The warm spray of water was comforting. She sat beneath it until it began to cool. Her strength returning bit by bit, she stood on wobbly legs and cleansed her body.

By the time she'd finished the water was cold, but she paid no attention. Her chest ached with a sense of betrayal she could not recall. The shattering pain in her head had finally subsided and her stomach had calmed.

She looked at her reflection again as she dried her hair. The woman in the mirror was at once familiar and alien. She remembered a great many things about herself, but none of the snippets connected or added up.

Vince was the key. He knew the truth. She felt it all the way to her bones.

But why was he hiding the truth from her?

That nagging sense of betrayal nudged her. Maybe she didn't know him as well as she thought. Maybe she couldn't trust him. She shook her head. That couldn't be right. Phil couldn't be right.

She wouldn't believe that.

Not yet anyway.

VINCE PULLED ON the clothes he'd worn the day before. Kat was already dressed and waiting. She was tense and remote. He didn't like the possibility that their love-making had done this to her. He held back the sigh that crept into his throat. Hurting her was his only regret. What happened between them only reinforced the reality that she was the only woman he'd ever loved. He would never love another.

If there had ever been any question, there was none now.

"Would you like to stop for breakfast?" he asked, breaking the long silence and hoping to lighten her somber mood.

She shook her head. "We need to get back."

He nodded. "All right."

Vince drove back to the house, Kat perched stiffly behind him. Dammit, he wished he knew what was bothering her. He wanted to ask but she'd made it very clear she didn't want to talk.

Once he'd parked, she slid off the bike and hurried inside as if she didn't want to be alone with him another second.

He exhaled a disgusted breath, then swore as he swung off the bike. He was sore as hell this morning. An irritating tick had started in his jaw. He didn't relish the thought of going inside, but he had no choice. He'd considered all his options and decided to play along with Yu's little power trip. They were getting down to the wire now, Vince needed to remain a part of the operation, not get left out for failing to show the proper ration of respect to their fearless leader.

Yeah, right. So fearless he cheated to make his point.

When Vince entered the house, the scene in the living room stopped him cold.

Will was screaming and writhing in pain on the couch. Leva and Kat hovered over him. Jamal paced back and forth, cursing every breath. Yu stood in the middle of it all staring down at Will with a homicidal glower.

"What's going on?"

No one bothered to answer Vince's question. Or maybe no one heard him, considering the ruckus.

Yu glared at Vince when he stopped on the fringes of the scene, then turned his attention back to Will. "I should kill you right now and get it over with," he threatened, his voice shaking with anger. "You have put the whole mission at risk."

Kat glanced up and caught Vince's eye. "He got

involved with the wrong people last night. Things went downhill between two of the dopeheads and Will was wounded in the ensuing exchange."

Will screeched in agony. "I can't feel my arm."

Kat shook her head and to Yu said, "He needs a hospital. We can't handle this kind of injury with a first-aid kit."

From the looks of his shirt and the couch beneath him, he'd been lying there bleeding for a good long while already. And Vince thought he'd had a rough night.

"No!" Yu roared. "All gunshot wounds are reported to the police. They'll take him into custody. We can't take that risk."

"And if he dies," Kat retorted, her expression hard, unflinching. "Where will we be the next time we need to breach high-tech security?"

Vince had to look away. What had they done to her? She acted just like one of *them*. Fear the likes of which he'd never before experienced gripped him. All undercover agents strove to make their cover real, but this went beyond that. What if this whole implant thing screwed up her head in a way that couldn't be undone? He blinked back a wave of emotion. He had the sudden overwhelming urge to go find Damrus and kill him. No, he told himself. Kat had proven by saving that guard that the implant hadn't overridden her basic human compassion. He wouldn't believe she'd turned that cold.

"You and Leva do what you can. If he dies," Yu added, looking from Kat to Leva, "well, you know what that means."

No one said a word.

Will writhed, moaning as much from the fear as the pain. The kid looked scared to death. If they didn't stop the bleeding, he probably would die. With the numbness there was a good chance irreparable nerve damage had occurred. There was nothing Vince could do about that. But he could patch him up. He knew how to do that. He'd had the same training as Kat, maybe more.

"Clear the table and get him on it," he ordered.

Everyone stopped whatever they were doing or thinking and stared at Vince.

"I'll need the sharpest knife you've got. Needle-nose pliers. The strongest thread and the largest sewing needle you can put your hands on."

Leva and Kat cleared the table without question. Jamal and Yu moved Will to the table, ignoring his weakening cries.

Vince put a hand on Kat's arm. "Sterilize the stuff the best you can."

She nodded.

"I'll have to make a run for the needle and thread," Leva said as she handed Vince the stack of clean white T-shirts she'd already gathered for bandages.

Vince noted a hint of distress in her voice. He was surprised. He didn't think she was capable of human emotion. Then again, he had to keep reminding himself that she, as well as the others, thought they were the good guys. "Large sewing needle and some tough thread," he reminded her, then added, "Hurry!"

"What else do we need?" Yu asked from right beside Vince.

Another surprise.

"Something to dull the pain, at least on a conscious level." Poor bastard had already suffered enough.

Jamal nodded. "I got just the thing." He disappeared and came back moments later with a bottle of high-octane gin.

Vince shrugged. "That'll do."

Keeping pressure on the wound to slow the bleeding, the three worked together to get as much of the gin into Will as Vince deemed necessary.

"This is the best I could do." Kat placed a razor-sharp paring knife and a freshly scrubbed pair of needle-nose pliers on the table next to Will's shoulder.

Vince allowed Yu to take over with keeping the pressure on the bandage while he washed his hands thoroughly.

When he returned to the table, all eyes looked at him expectantly. Except for Will, of course, he'd already slipped into an alcohol-induced coma.

"This is going to take a few minutes. As soon as Leva gets back we'll need to try to close this wound."

Yu nodded. "What do you need us to do?"

Vince looked at Will then back at Yu. "Hold him down. He looks out of it, but I guarantee he'll feel this."

From the opposite side of the table, Yu pinned Vince with a questioning look. "You've done this before?"

Vince knew he wasn't asking out of concern for Will's life. "Once."

There was no exit wound, which meant the bullet had lodged somewhere inside. The neat entry path went straight to the bone where the bullet had lodged. It had torn through muscle and ligament to make its path. The damage was not so extensive to the naked eye, but Vince had enough training to recognize it was worse than it looked. Since the bullet was easily accessible, he had no qualms about removing it. Considering it might be more than twenty-four hours before the kid got the proper medical attention, if he got any at all. As Vince had anticipated, Will had to be restrained.

By the time Vince had removed the bullet, which thankfully was intact, and cleaned up the wound, Leva had returned and Will was unconscious again. Vince hadn't seen any bone fragments lying around. Hopefully there weren't any.

Leva quickly sterilized the needle using the gin. If what they'd done so far didn't kill the kid, he doubted that would, either. The seam job wasn't half bad. It had been a while since he'd had the training or the need to use it, but at least the bleeding had stopped.

Kat applied antibiotic ointment and bandaged the wound. It amazed Vince that Leva'd had the foresight to get proper bandages and over-the-counter antibiotic cream.

The whole group looked haggard. For the first time since this began, Vince realized how lost and alone this group of kids was. Though his sympathy only went so far with some—he glanced at Leva and then Yu—still they had been preyed upon by a manipulative and evil man and his organization.

One way or another Vince had to see that Kovner was stopped.

He looked at Kat then. She was beat. Guilt plagued him again. As much as his brain knew last night had been a mistake, his heart simply wouldn't admit it.

"If his arm remains paralyzed," Yu said, stepping forward to claim Vince's full attention, "you will take his place on the mission." Yu offered him a tight, fake smile. "Perhaps you will have your uses, after all, Ferrelli."

"And what about Will?" Vince asked when Yu would have turned away.

A look that was more telling than his words settled on Vince. "He made a mistake. Put all of us at risk. His fate is yet to be determined."

"In other words," Vince pressed, "if he's outlived his usefulness, you'll kill him."

All eyes were on Yu now.

He smirked. "Have we learned nothing about respect, my friend?"

As if to remind Vince, his head throbbed and his side ached. Oh, he'd learned about respect, all right, but not from Philip Yu.

During the next twenty-four hours Yu would learn a great many things and, if he was lucky, he'd live to glean wisdom from the experience.

Chapter Twelve

"What if they have a secondary you don't know about and it sets off the alarm?" Vince asked after listening to Will's overview of the electronic security maintained at the target site. He still had no real information regarding the actual target. The schematics weren't that telling; could be the floor plans for any large building anywhere.

"There's no way they could hide it," Will insisted. "Nothing is invisible if you know what to look for."

Will looked tired, his features drawn with the intensity of the pain no doubt nagging at him. After Vince had patched him up, he'd slept for hours. The moment he'd awakened, just after dusk, Yu had demanded that he get to work. When it became obvious he hadn't regained any use of his right arm, he'd been ordered to bring Vince up to speed on how to handle the program, which was essential to the team's mission. Without Will's program to shut down security and remote surveillance, no one was going in. The whole strike had been planned around Will's ability to get them in and out without detection.

Will glanced around covertly, then leaned closer to Vince. "Look, man, if you master this, I'm dead."

Absolute fear stared at him from those bloodshot eyes. Vince lifted a skeptical eyebrow. "And if I don't, what happens to me?"

Will looked away.

"How are we doing?" Yu left his hushed conversation with Leva and Kat and stalked toward the two men as if sensing the sudden change in subject matter at the table.

Vince could feel the intensity of Will's gaze on him. "I don't know," Vince hedged. "I have no problem maneuvering the program, but considering how little time we have to prepare, I don't trust myself to retain all the solutions to possible problems that could occur."

"What are you saying?" Yu demanded, his impatience and frustration showing.

Vince shrugged. "I'm saying we need Will on site. He can watch over my shoulder and keep me straight."

Anger tightened Yu's features. "You're proving an extreme disappointment, Ferrelli."

He laughed. "No one could know this program the way Will does," he countered. "He designed it." Vince leaned back in his chair and folded his arms across his chest. "You know what I think? I think you're looking for a reason to be disappointed. That gives you reason enough to be rid of me."

Kat and Leva had stopped talking and were listening to the tense exchange. Vince had counted on that. That vein in Yu's forehead that always throbbed when he was royally pissed, bulged now.

Knowing nothing else would work, Yu turned the tables on Vince. "This part of the mission is essential. There is no alternative. If due to an infection or other complication Will is unable to guide you, we need you to be prepared. Do you not understand the significance of reducing all possible risks?"

Vince understood, all right. He got up, going nose to nose with Yu. "If I'm so valuable to the mission now, then why am I still in the dark about the target?" He needed that information. He needed it now while he still had time to pass it along to Callahan.

Yu merely looked at him with mounting indifference and utter disdain. "You will be briefed at noon tomorrow before we go in."

That wouldn't work. No way. He had to know now. Vince threw his hands up and backed away from the table and Will. "Forget it. If you can't trust me now, then I'm out. J-Man can work with Will. He won't have anything to do but wait behind the wheel anyway."

"Hell, no!" Jamal shouted, popping up from the couch and lumbering in their direction. "I don't know jack about that program or computers and don't have no hankerin' to learn. Forget it, Phil. I ain't doing it." He punctuated his statement with exaggerated body language that included a dramatic wag of his head. "I'm a wheelman. Keep an extra weapon taped under the dash when I'm driving. I'm ready for anything, but I ain't doing that."

Yu's gaze remained locked with Vince's, the fury blazing into a maniacal glower. He visibly shook with the strain of maintaining his cool. He wanted to kill Vince. Yet, when he spoke his tone was surprisingly calm.

"We need a moment."

Yu made a dismissive gesture. The room cleared immediately. Kat glanced back at Vince as she and Leva headed for the basement. Vince couldn't read the look. She'd barely spoken to him since they'd left the motel. They needed to talk about last night. He had to know where they stood.

Yu moved to the other side of the room and sat in the chair Kat had vacated. He motioned for Vince to take the other. He clocked Vince's every move, his gaze never leaving him.

"I don't trust you, Ferrelli," he said frankly.

Vince relaxed fully into the upholstered chair. "If it makes you feel any better, I don't trust you, either."

"But," Yu allowed, "this team needs you. For now," he added pointedly. "Since Kat trusts you and you appear willing to risk her life considering she vouched for you, I'm willing to take the risk, as well."

Vince didn't believe for one minute Yu would harm Kat, not physically anyway. He wanted her too badly. Anything negative he could find out about Vince would be to his advantage. He would use it to force Kat into submission. *We had a deal*...Kat and Yu had a deal. Vince's gut told him that it all hinged on him. But Vince wasn't foolish enough to believe that Kat would be safe simply because Yu had a thing for her. Kovner, The

Man, would have the final say. And though WSA had allowed Yu to walk away from his last major mission for them, the odds were against any of the team's survival. When they had served their usefulness, they would be eliminated. No loose ends. No one was indispensable. Sadly, twenty-somethings with a burning desire to belong and to achieve, such as Yu and the others, were easy to find.

"It's about time," Vince responded to Yu's reluctant agreement to fill him in. "Trust is good for morale," he added sportingly.

Yu didn't look amused, but he carried on, anyway. "Tomorrow at noon there will be a memorial service at the Church of the Incarnation, it's on Eastern Avenue in D.C. Immediately following the service a reception will be held at a nearby hotel for foreign VIPs in attendance. The penthouse, where the reception will be held, is our target. Tomorrow's performance is especially important for more reasons than one. We have an audience of one who wants a front-row seat."

That meant Kovner would be there. "The Man?" Vince inquired casually.

Yu nodded. "Who else?"

Vince swallowed tightly. Kovner's appearance was what they'd hoped for. That meant they had to let this thing play out until the last minutes. It also meant a lot of collateral damage if anything went wrong. A sinking feeling accompanied that realization. "The security on those schematics looks a little sophisticated for a hotel," Vince noted, fishing.

A shrug of indifference lifted one of Yu's shoulders. "The hotel security has been beefed up for this reception. They're not taking any chances."

"One of the foreign VIPs is the target," Vince probed.

Yu smiled knowingly. "The target is someone who is very close to the President and is passing along secrets to this country's archenemy. Someone leaking the secrets shared during trusted intimacy."

Vince went still. He couldn't mean…

"Our target is the First Lady."

MIDNIGHT HAD COME and gone and still Kat couldn't sleep. She didn't toss and turn, though. She lay perfectly still, forcing her respiration to remain even and deep.

Vince wasn't asleep, either. But he pretended to be…just as she did.

Kat squeezed her eyes shut and tried to block the barrage of memories that simply would not stay away no matter how hard she tried to keep them at bay. Anger surged through her each time the conflicting images and words clashed. She didn't know what it all meant. Just when she'd thought she knew who she was, everything became even more confusing. There was one thing she knew with complete certainty: she could trust no one.

Not the man lying next to her or the others on her team. All had lied to her…betrayed her in one way or another. She sensed it with absolute certainty.

But it was Vince's betrayal that went the deepest. Every fiber of her being cried out with the old ache…an ache she couldn't fully remember.

She forced herself to relax again and pushed the thoughts away. She had a job to do. Nothing or no one was going to stop her. Last night's intense lovemaking filtered through the wall she'd erected in her mind. The sensations weakened her resolve, made her want to reach out to the man beside her. She couldn't afford to trust him…knew he had somehow betrayed her, but he owned her heart. She wanted to laugh and cry at the same time. She loved him. There was no question. She felt it as strongly as she'd ever felt anything in her life.

Just her luck to fall in love with the kind of man she couldn't trust.

Phil had told her what he'd done. He still didn't trust Vince. So he'd baited him, set Vince up just to see if he'd betray them. Kat thanked God that it appeared he wasn't going to make a move with the information. By morning it would be too late. Phil wouldn't allow anyone out of his sight during the final hours.

Despite the knowledge that Vince had somehow betrayed her deeply, she didn't want Phil to be right. She didn't want Vince to die. Every passing minute without any wrong moves out of Vince served to disprove Phil's theory.

Vince may have betrayed her somehow in the past on a personal level, but he was not a traitor. He wouldn't risk her life.

No sooner than her weary mind completed the thought, he moved. Sat up, then waited to see if she would stir.

Kat's heart shuddered, then sank. God, don't let him do this.

She lay perfectly still, waiting, listening.

Vince quietly pulled on his clothes without the aid of light, then slipped across the room. She didn't have to open her eyes to know he'd paused at the door to look back at her.

Then he was gone.

All hope vanished with him.

VINCE STEPPED OUT into the dark night and scanned the area. He spotted Callahan's SUV a couple houses down. He walked in that direction, ignoring the loud music and lively shouts of partyers coming from various houses along the block. The people next door were really tearing the house down.

Callahan picked up his movement and met him on the sidewalk. They walked leisurely across the closest lawn and into the backyard of the neighboring house. Heavy cloud cover allowed for near-complete darkness. Vince appreciated that luxury. Slipping out of the house was a risk in itself, he damn sure couldn't afford to be caught talking to Callahan. But he had to relay the intel Yu had given him.

Intel that still startled him.

Callahan leaned against a tree truck and waited for him to come closer. "Whatcha got?"

Vince carefully relayed the details of tomorrow's strike.

"You're kidding, right?"

Vince shook his head, then remembered she wouldn't be able to see him in the darkness. "No. This is way beyond the scope of what we expected."

"No joke. Casey's going to freak out. He'll have to notify the Secret Service and they'll call in the ATF."

Vince rubbed a hand over his face. "You don't know how much I'd like to pull the plug on this here and now." He blew out a weary breath. "But Kovner is making a personal appearance." He sighed. "Still, something doesn't feel right about it."

"So you're not so sure about this?"

"Yu told me himself. But the elaborate security system shown on the schematics just doesn't jive with the target. But if we want Kovner we're going to have to let this thing play out down to the wire and find out if Yu is on the up-and-up."

"If Casey sees it differently, they'll pull you out and take Yu and his team down," she said, putting voice to what he already knew.

"I'll be ready either way."

"And Kat?" Callahan wanted to know. "That's under control?"

"Yeah. I'll take care of Kat."

"By the way," she said, "about that bank account in the Caymans. It wasn't easy Lucas said, but they traced it to Kovner. He transfers money to a bank here in Port Charlotte presumably for supporting the team and their efforts."

Vince nodded. "I figured as much. Yu had to be getting the money siphoned to him from somewhere."

When Callahan pushed off from the tree, Vince caught a glimpse of light or a glow. "What's that?" He moved closer to her, staring at her chest.

"It's nothing," she protested, annoyance in her voice.

Since his eyes had adjusted to the darkness he could vaguely make out her face, but little else. Her blond hair was tucked under a black baseball cap, the bill facing backward. Her jeans were black as was her hooded sweatshirt. Still, when she'd moved, he'd noticed something, a glimmer or something where the sweatshirt zipped in front.

"It's not nothing," he said pointedly. "Now, what gives?"

She huffed, then walked up to him and pulled her sweatshirt away from her chest so that he could see. Beneath the sweatshirt she wore a plain black T-shirt, but that wasn't what had snagged his attention. Around her neck hung a dogtag chain and on the chain was a small, military-issue light stick.

"Are you satisfied?" she hissed.

He still didn't get it. "What—" Then it hit him. "You're afraid of the dark."

"Get lost, Ferrelli," she muttered. "I got places to go and calls to make."

"Wait." He caught her by the arm when she would have walked past him. His overdeveloped sense of caution had caused him to humiliate her. "I'm sorry, I didn't mean anything." Big, bad Callahan was afraid of the dark. He fought away the smile, forced the amusement out of his voice. She had her Achilles' heel, after all. "It's okay. Really. We all have our weaknesses."

"Yeah, right." She stabbed a finger in his chest. "You just remember to keep your mouth shut or I'll kick your—"

"I get the picture," he interjected. There were few females in Mission Recovery. Those few had to work extra hard for respect. It wasn't fair, it just was. Not quite like what Kat had suffered from the Navy—and him, he amended. The memory seared him like a hot poker. "Don't worry, your secret is safe with me," he assured Callahan, pushing away the painful memories of the past.

She trudged off without acknowledging his pledge of secrecy. Vince shook his head. It was hard to believe that Blue Callahan was afraid of anything, much less something as harmless as the dark.

Like he'd told her, no one would ever hear it from him.

He glanced down the street at the house where Kat slept. Now all he had to do was get back in without being caught.

KAT MOVED QUICKLY through the darkness. She hadn't waited around to hear the final departing words between Vince and the woman. Disappointment and anger burned in Kat's chest. She'd trusted Vince. Bet her life on him when she vouched for his trustworthiness and insisted he be included on the team.

She'd made a mistake.

A tiny crack formed in her heart as she hurried to get back to their room before Vince did.

More confusing thoughts reeled through her mind. He was a traitor…but some part of her refused to acknowledge that truth. She'd heard him with her own ears. The Secret Service, the ATF. He was some kind of government undercover agent. One of those people who thought the WSA was the enemy. Something dark and just out of reach stirred deep inside her. She shook it off. She'd also heard Vince say he'd take care of her. A mixture of hurt and fear pumped through her veins. What was that supposed to mean?

She wanted so desperately for none of it to be true. But it was true.

There was no denying it any longer.

Vince was a traitor.

She began jerking off her clothes before she got all the way up the stairs. She threw the wadded bundle on the floor and slipped back into bed, immediately focusing on slowing her erratic respiration. Slow, deep breaths. He couldn't know that she hadn't been asleep this whole time. Couldn't suspect that she knew the truth.

Despite her best efforts her body tensed when he stole back into the room. She found herself holding her breath as his clothes landed on the floor, piece by piece. First the whisper of his shirt as he dragged it off his shoulders. Then the metal over metal sound of his zipper lowering…the brush of denim against flesh. Then he eased down next to her. She reminded herself to breathe. His arms worked their way around her and she forced her muscles to relax. He pulled her close to his chest. The steady pounding of his heart made her ache. She squeezed her eyes shut and fought the emotions that suddenly bombarded her.

God, she couldn't cry now. Not now. He'd know something was wrong. She had to distract herself… focus on anything else.

She snuggled in his arms and pretended to rouse from sleep. "Mmm," she purred, moving against him, feeling his body's instant response.

"Mmm, yourself," he murmured close to her ear.

She felt the bandage he still wore from the beating he'd suffered at the hands of Phil and Jamal. Her heart squeezed at the thought of his being hurt then, or tomorrow. She couldn't bear it. She loved him...

But he was a traitor.

"Kiss me," she ordered, her lips trembling.

He kissed her. Kissed her long and deep as only Vince Ferrelli could. No one touched her the way Vince did. Tonight he would touch her for the last time. Though she still couldn't name it, she knew he had betrayed her once before. She also knew that he'd used her this time to get close to the others, to infiltrate this team.

And Kat knew what she had to do.

Phil would be waiting for her report.

But that could wait a few hours more.

Vince sank into her, forcing all thought save one from her mind. She loved him and she wanted this last night with him.

Much later, sated by the lovemaking and emotionally drained by the night's hope-shattering revelations, Kat fell asleep. She dreamed vividly. Dreamed of Vince... and another woman...a woman who looked just like her, but somehow wasn't her. He whispered sweet words to her...told her he'd missed her. Missed her and then some.

Kat jerked awake just before dawn.

She listened, lay perfectly still. The sound of Vince's even, deep breathing…the feel of his heart beating steadily in his chest…the strength of his arms around her.

And then she knew.

Chapter Thirteen

"Let's run through this one last time," Yu ordered. "There can be no mistakes."

He paced like a caged lion.

He was nervous.

Vince watched him closely, but Yu was careful to avoid eye contact. Vince had a bad feeling about that. He glanced at Kat across the table. She was distant and preoccupied again today. The only time he'd felt close to her in the past twenty-four hours was when they'd made love after midnight. And even then there had been a desperation about her...a sadness almost. He couldn't shake the feeling that something was troubling her. The implant was his best guess. But he couldn't deny the possibility that their lovemaking had brought back old hurts and insecurities. Maybe she'd remembered just enough to realize he'd somehow betrayed her.

Whatever it was, she refused to talk about it. She didn't talk about anything except the mission.

Empty fast-food containers and wrappers were scattered on the table. Vince pushed the remains of his barely touched breakfast aside and pulled the laptop close. Will didn't bother to get up from the couch and come over.

The kid looked like death warmed over today. His face was flushed and feverish, he probably needed prescription antibiotics. Not to mention a doctor and, in all likelihood, a neurosurgeon. His arm was still immobile. If his fever worsened he would be no help to Vince, but that wasn't really a problem. Vince had the system nailed down—at least for this mission. Unless there was a glitch, he wasn't worried.

Not that the mission was going down, anyway. By now an entire SWAT force of Mission Recovery Specialists would be in place at the hotel. Yu's team didn't have a snowball's chance in hell of completing their mission. The moment Kovner showed up it would be over. Waiting out Kovner was the only reason Mission Recovery hadn't moved in already.

Leva placed two metal cases on the table and opened them, surveyed the contents, and said to Yu, "I'm ready." She closed the cases and waited expectantly.

Yu turned to Kat.

"I've selected one primary location and four secondary marks." Her gaze was flat, her expression unreadable. "The first explosion will take place behind the tabernacle to incite panic as well as to create a diversion from the real danger."

Vince went rigid. He looked from Kat to Yu as she continued without hesitation, as if planning destruction and the death of countless people was an everyday affair.

"A few will die in the first explosion," she said without emotion. "But most will only be shaken. They'll try to run, but there will only be a five-second delay before the secondary devices detonate. Each secondary is strategically placed where a pendentive supports the main dome. The force of the blast will shatter the supports and surrounding exterior wall for several feet on either side and the dome will collapse instantly, killing anyone who survives the fallout and expected chaos."

Yu smiled. "Perfect."

"Wait," Vince cut in sharply. His heart pumped adrenaline through his veins at an unparalleled rate. "I thought this was going down at the hotel." He gestured to the schematics on the laptop in front of him. "This isn't the layout for a church." A hard, cold reality gripped his gut.

"Sorry, bro," Will piped up from his position on the couch. "I really like you, you know." He shrugged his one good shoulder. "But I did what I had to do." A grin slid across his pain-weary face. "I played the scared-for-my-life part pretty damn good, didn't I?"

"You'll play the *dead* part even better." Yu put two rounds in his chest.

Kat lunged to her feet, sending her chair clattering to the floor. "You didn't have to do that." This time there was no missing the ferocity in her tone as well as her expression. "You didn't have to kill him."

"He had outlived his purpose." Putting his weapon away, Yu turned to Vince. "To answer your question, there's been a change in plans." To Jamal, he said, "We leave in five minutes."

Vince considered going for his gun and stopping this now, but that would be a mistake. He had his orders. He glanced at Kat, who was still glowering at Yu. The one thing he had to do was to stay close to her. He desperately wished he could read her mind right now.

Leva and Jamal took the cases away, presumably to load them into one of the SUVs, while Yu disappeared into the basement. Probably taking a last look around Leva's shop to see if they'd forgotten anything they might need.

Vince seized what would probably be the only moment he would have alone with Kat. "This isn't right," he said, infusing a sense of desperation into his tone that wasn't far off the mark of what he really felt. He glanced over at Will. "Will didn't have to die."

Kat fastened a black utility belt around her waist. The utility belt contained the items she would need to secure the devices in place. They were all wearing the usual garb, black cargo pants, boots and long-sleeved T-shirts. The ski masks would come later.

"It was the best for the team," she said without looking at him. "Otherwise Phil wouldn't have done it."

Vince's jaw tightened. This wasn't the real Kat talking. There was no one around to keep her from saying what she really felt. Vince didn't like this. She'd risked her life to save that guard, suddenly Will's death was "the best for the team." He had to seriously consider that she might have finally gone over the edge, her senses overrun by an experimental device that was probably going to get her killed. He thought about the pills Damrus had given him, but quickly dismissed that idea. Too risky. Even Damrus had thought so.

"I can't believe you'd think that," he murmured. This had gone too far. It was one thing to maintain a cover, but a total loss of basic human compassion was another thing altogether. The implant had really scrambled her logic.

She slapped a clip into her weapon, shoved it into her belt and stared up at him with eyes so empty he could scarcely bare to look.

"Maybe you don't know me as well as you think, *Vinny.*"

There was a hardness about her voice when she said his name, a hardness punctuated by a flicker of ice in that dull gaze.

He wanted to say more, but Yu came in just then. "Everything's set. Let's go," he ordered, glancing from one to the other, then heading for the door.

It was raining when they left, but the precipitation slowed, eventually stopping altogether as they drove northward, toward the nation's capital. Kat drove the SUV, Yu sat in the back, leaving Vince the passenger seat next to Kat. Leva and Jamal were behind them in the second SUV.

Years of training had sharpened Vince's instincts to an inordinately heightened level. Those instincts were screaming at him now. The sudden change in plans. Eliminating Will. The road signs as they neared D.C. proper.

A church wouldn't have a complicated electronic security system, certainly not one that would need over-riding in the middle of the day on a Sunday. They hadn't needed Will at all this time. The whole hoopla over his injury and his importance to the mission had been a farce to fool Vince, to make him feel as if he were finally in. He wondered if Kat had been in on it from the beginning and if Yu realized that even if his team was somehow successful, that they would all die anyway. Kovner would not leave any loose ends unless it served his purpose.

All things considered, if they didn't need Will anymore, they damn sure didn't need Vince. This was the reason Yu had chosen to sit in the back seat. He wanted to be able to keep an eye on Vince.

Kat took the New York Avenue/U.S. 50 exit. Vince mentally pictured the streets of D.C. and was certain they should have taken the I-295 south exit, then Pennsylvania Avenue. Why take an indirect route?

Vince resisted the urge to look behind him. Callahan would be back there somewhere, reporting the discrepancy in their route. More than likely the ATF had someone on their tail, as well, since they were carrying explosives.

Still, something more nagged at Vince.

At the last second, Kat wheeled the SUV into the parking lot of a premier hotel located only blocks from Capitol Hill.

"Why are we stopping here?" Vince's voice sounded loud and harsh after the long minutes of tense silence.

Kat glanced at him as she shifted into park. "Just a precaution, Vince. You know the drill."

He clutched her hand in his when she would have gotten out. Yu was already standing outside the SUV near Vince's door. Vince stared directly into her eyes, willing her to see the depth of his concern. "I know the drill. Do you?"

"Gut check, Vince," she said, her expression giving nothing away. "Trust is essential. You know that, too."

She got out…slammed the door behind her.

His respiration increased tenfold. Hope sprouted, but some part of him wouldn't let him trust mere words. Words, phrases that only the real Kat would know, held significance for him. For anyone who'd survived BUDS training.

Yu tapped on his window. Vince stepped back into character and emerged from the vehicle. He glared at Yu. "This is crap. You know that. Why didn't you just do me at the house like you did Will? Why the games?"

"You have a command performance, Ferrelli. Haven't you figured that out already?" Yu took Vince's weapon and tossed it into the nearby shrubbery. He inclined his head toward the side entrance through which Kat had already disappeared. "Let's go."

Inside the hotel they moved through a number of doors marked Staff Only until they reached a locker room utilized by kitchen staff. Jamal and Leva were already there. A white uniform covered Leva's dark clothing. Another man appeared, this one wearing a name tag, apron and chef's hat that marked him as a member of the hotel kitchen staff. He led the way to a large storage area. A rear service door stood open. A white van with the hotel logo on both sides was backed up to the open door.

The hotel employee nodded then disappeared. Jamal opened the rear doors of the van and Leva climbed in, followed by Kat. Yu pushed Vince forward. "Inside," he snarled.

Leva donned a chef's hat, one exactly like the hotel employee had worn, and slid behind the wheel while Vince and the others remained out of sight in the cargo area of the van.

As she drove away from the building Vince noticed the two metal cases on the floor. A rising sense of panic made it difficult for him to breathe. Oh, no.

"The others were decoys," Yu told him, noticing the direction of his gaze. "They'll keep your friends busy for a little while since they look just like the real thing and a timer will be counting down."

He shook his head at Vince. "You didn't think we'd be stupid enough to forego added precautions, did you?"

Yes, he had.

Vince had assumed that since they'd done the ICS job straight-up with no smoke and mirrors, that they would this one, as well. There had been no reason—no indication whatsoever—to suspect otherwise. Vince had failed to see it coming. He'd allowed personal feelings to get in the way of his better judgment.

Big mistake.

He should have known that if Kovner was going to put in an appearance there would be extra measures taken to ensure a wide safety net.

Jamal climbed into the passenger seat next to Leva, giving her additional directions instead of playing his usual role as driver.

"You and your people thought you were one step ahead of us," Yu bragged. "But all along, you were one step behind. I never trusted you from the beginning."

Yu gave himself too much credit. He wasn't that smart. "What gave me away?" Vince asked archly. "We both know it wasn't your superior intelligence."

Fury tightened Yu's Asian features. "The question is not what, it's who."

Vince blinked. His gaze instantly sought Kat, who looked away without flinching.

"She followed you. Reported every word back to me." Yu laughed dryly. "Though she did skim over the part about her methods of distraction after the fact."

Vince refused to believe that Kat had turned on him completely. There had to be an explanation. He swallowed the rock of emotion in his throat. Or maybe he was a bigger fool than even he realized.

He had to focus. Vince brutally pushed away the self-deprecating thoughts. In fact he cleared his mind of everything except the burning desire to exact revenge on Yu. "It's not over," he told him, his lethal tone conveying the depth of his confidence.

Yu laughed. "You're wrong, my friend." He nodded to Kat. "Pat him down and make sure I didn't miss anything." To Vince he added, "For you it's over in more ways than you know."

Kat's hands moved over his body, her gaze focused

on the task. Her fingers stilled on the backup piece tucked into his athletic tube sock. She arched an eyebrow and glanced at Yu. "I guess you missed this." She removed the weapon and tossed it on the far side of the van.

Vince watched intently for the opportunity to meet her gaze. He desperately wanted another reading on her. She moved away without looking at him. He bit back the words he wanted to say. He couldn't give her away. Even if she'd compromised him, he couldn't do the same to her. The Kat he had once known would never have risked his life for revenge. But maybe he didn't know this Kat, implant aside. Maybe that's why he'd been her Romeo profile. Maybe she'd waited four long years to have her chance at revenge.

Vince looked away from her. He wouldn't believe that.

The vehicle slowed, then bounced over a dip. They'd left the street, but Vince couldn't see where they were since there were no windows in the cargo area. Leva guided the van around what he presumed to be a parking lot, then stopped at an entrance.

A carwash.

While the automatic system went through its cycles, Leva moved from the driver's seat and discarded the white uniform and hat. Jamal slid into the seat she'd vacated. He immediately leaned forward and fiddled under the dash while Leva opened the metal cases. She nodded to Yu, affirming a go-ahead.

Kat sat solemnly by, not saying a word, still denying Vince eye contact. He turned his attention to Yu and considered taking him. He knew he could, but he wouldn't risk Kat's getting injured in the ensuing struggle.

Vince wondered briefly how long it would take Callahan and the ATF to realize they were gone. Callahan would put in a call to Lucas. The ATF would waste precious time defusing the decoys back at the hotel. But Callahan wouldn't be so easily distracted, she would be considering the traffic she'd seen leave the hotel parking lot in the few minutes after the team disappeared inside the hotel. It wouldn't take her long to surmise that the hotel van she'd watched depart was the vehicle she needed to try to find. She was quick on her feet. She'd call in her suspicions and half the D.C. police force would be looking for the van with the hotel logo.

As the carwash completed its cycle, Vince realized the significance of this seeming waste of time. They'd just washed off the logo.

As the van eased out of the tunnel, Yu confirmed that last thought. "This van was especially prepared using a paint that would wash off under exposure to high-pressure water spray. So, you see, even if the rain had continued, it wouldn't have interfered. Impressive, don't you agree?"

"Too bad you weren't the mastermind who thought of it," Vince guessed. Yu's murderous look told him he was right. Philip Yu was smart, calculating even, but he wasn't that good. Not yet. If Vince had his way, he never would be. His rise to the criminal cream of the crop would end today.

"Like I said before," Vince commented, adding insult to injury, "it's not over."

Yu relaxed against the cargo area's exterior wall as the van eased back into the thin traffic. At this time of morning on a Sunday, most people were at one of two places, home or church.

"Let me tell you just how over it is," Yu offered smugly.

Vince shrugged. "Suit yourself."

Kat stared straight ahead, choosing to ignore the whole conversation as well as the situation. Vince wanted to believe that she would somehow come through for him before this was over…but he couldn't be sure. He wanted to believe that what she'd said to him earlier about trust being essential was her way of letting him know that she had everything under control. Dammit, he couldn't know for sure. If that damned implant hadn't been wreaking such havoc, headaches, confusion and all, he might let himself believe. As it was, he couldn't count on anything. Especially considering that she was the one to give him up. That idea burned in his gut. She'd followed him, then reported back to Yu—after making love to Vince.

Then he remembered the desperation, the sadness when they'd made love. Just something else he'd missed. All the warning signs had been there, he'd simply been too blinded by personal feelings to see.

"You think you have an ace up your sleeve," Yu began, enjoying immensely that he appeared to know something else Vince didn't. "But you're wrong."

He braced the hand holding the weapon he had aimed at Vince on his bent knee and continued. "You see we allowed your friend—" his brow lined in concentration

"—Callahan, I believe is her name. Anyway, we allowed her to go back to her vehicle and make contact with your people before I, personally, intercepted her."

Equal parts fear and fury speared through Vince's chest. "Where is she?" he demanded, coming up off the floor.

The butt of Yu's weapon connected with Vince's forehead right where Kat had taped his previous injury. Pain splintered inside his skull, but he ignored it.

The nose of the weapon bore into his sternum then. "Sit down or you'll be making that command performance on your back with a hole in your chest."

Vince gritted his teeth against the rage that all but consumed him. Forcing himself to comply with Yu's demand, he sat down. As long as he was alive there was a chance he could stop this—with or without Kat's help. "What did you do to Callahan, you sick—"

"He didn't kill her," Kat said suddenly, a twinge of desperation in her voice.

"Yet," Yu contributed.

"Where is she?" Vince had to know. Had to find a way to help her. Blood trickled into his eye, he scrubbed it away, no longer feeling the pain…no longer feeling anything but the vile hunger for revenge.

Philip Yu was a dead man.

Whatever else happened, Vince would see to that.

"She's all tied up, shall we say." Yu smirked. "We couldn't risk leaving any evidence so we set one of Leva's premiere devices in her shop. I don't think there will be much left for forensics to work with back at the house."

Before Vince could ask again where Callahan was,

Yu resumed his arrogant monologue. "Oh, and your friend, Callahan." Yu smiled slyly. "Very nice eyes. More blue than any I've ever seen." He sighed wistfully. "Well, she's in the shop waiting for the fireworks." He checked his watch. "In just under one hour she'll see firsthand what an amazing demolitions designer Leva is."

Vince looked directly into Yu's eyes, allowing him to see all that he didn't bother to say. Yu flinched. Vince smiled.

"Did you leave the light on?" Vince's voice was gruff and as hard and unyielding as granite.

Yu scowled at him, clearly shaken by the eye contact. "What?"

"Did you leave the light on in the shop?" he repeated, grinding out the words. With no windows in the basement, Leva's shop would be as dark as a cave. *You're afraid of the dark.* Callahan would be terrified.

"No I didn't leave the light on. What difference does it make? You think your little friend is going to care. She's too busy watching the L.E.D. display count down the seconds and minutes until…*boom.*" Yu waved his arms magnanimously then laughed at Vince's glare. "What do you care, Ferrelli? You'll already be dead by then."

Chapter Fourteen

The van rolled to a stop in the service parking area. The main parking lot was still all but empty. Kat glanced at her watch. In just half an hour that same lot would be jam-packed with regular attendees and tourists. Her heart rate hadn't slowed since waking this morning. Her hands shook slightly.

She had to focus. It was the only way to get this done. No way could she look at Vince. She'd lose it if she did.

He'd brought this on himself. Traitors weren't willingly abided under in any circumstances. She knew too well from personal experience.

None of that mattered right now.

She couldn't allow her thoughts to wander even for a moment. Her emotions had shut down hours ago. She functioned now purely on instinct.

She had a job to do.

Nothing was going to stop her.

Leva pulled on her ski mask. "You ready?"

Kat nodded. "Let's do it."

When she pushed up to slide between the seats, Vince manacled her wrist and pulled her to him.

"Let her go," Yu demanded, the sound of his weapon engaging echoed in the cargo area.

Ignoring Yu, the fingers of Vince's other hand knotted in her hair; he forced her to look at him. "I'll be waiting for you, Kat, to come rescue me." He kissed her with an intensity of feeling that took her breath, then he released her.

Kat scrambled free of his hold, her heart racing even harder, her skin suddenly damp with perspiration.

As she sidled between the seats she heard the smack of a hard fist against flesh and Vince's answering groan. She set her jaw hard and looked back one last time. When Vince had shaken off the pain that no doubt followed the blow, his gaze locked with hers.

"Don't hold your breath, Ferrelli," she told him. "It pays to be a winner. You should remember that."

Outside the van, Kat pulled on her ski mask and took one of the metal cases from Leva. Without speaking, the two ducked into the thick copse of deciduous trees surrounding the courtyard of Mary's Garden.

Not only had Vince been given the wrong information about the hotel, the church had been wrong, as well. Oh, there was definitely a noon memorial service at the other place, at which the First Lady would be in attendance.

But she wasn't their target.

Their target was the Israeli ambassador to the United States. Today at noon mass, despite his own personal religious beliefs, he would be in attendance at a small service for a close American friend. A nobody in the greater scheme of things. There would be little security and certainly no pre-arrival checks. The ambassador's personal security would be in attendance with him, but no one else. He was an open target.

Kat didn't know all the details as to why the ambassador was a target; her best guess would be because he was a personal enemy of Kovner's. But Kovner had accused him of being a traitor. The ambassador's assassination was the whole reason for Kovner's in-the-flesh appearance today.

Inside one of the metal cases there was a high-tech video camera. Once planted near the entrance to the Blessed Sacrament Chapel, Kovner would be able to watch everything from the safety of the van.

Urns sitting atop stone piers and overflowing with flowers, all blooming white, marked the entrance to Mary's Garden. They moved along the outer perimeter, careful to stay in the shaded cover of the numerous shrubs and flowering trees. Kat caught a glimpse of a magnificent fountain and then a reflecting pool where a life-size statue of Mary and the baby Jesus stood. She looked away, squashing the sentimentality that sprouted.

She wasn't the sentimental type anymore. She was a woman with a mission.

But she prayed, anyway, nearly laughing at herself.

They entered the chapel and set immediately to work. Minutes whizzed by as Kat carefully placed the explosives. Leva worked to strategically mount the camera. Using a tiny, handheld two-way radio, Jamal kept her informed as to the reception quality and angle feeding to the monitor in the van.

They had just fifteen minutes to do their work.

Kat ignored the brilliant architecture and breathtaking beauty around her as she hoisted herself up to each destination. She could have set these charges for the desired outcome with one eye closed and one hand tied behind her back. It was all so simple. So elegantly simple.

And no one would see it coming…until it was too late.

With three minutes to spare Kat and Leva exited the chapel and again used the lovely landscape as efficient cover.

Kat stopped dead-still when a priest paused to admire the statue of Mary and Jesus. Leva grunted as she slammed into Kat's back. Kat nodded toward the priest. Leva bobbed her head in understanding.

The longest minute Kat had ever lived passed as they waited for the man to move on. The slightest crunch of a fallen leaf or the brush of rubber soles against perfectly manicured grass would not be good right now.

Kat didn't want the priest to die.

She doubted God forgave sins like that.

When the man finally strolled away, Kat let go the breath she'd been holding.

"It's clear," she whispered, and started forward.

"Wait a minute, Kat."

When Kat turned around she came nose to muzzle with Leva's Glock 9 mm. Somehow she wasn't surprised.

"Sorry, Kat woman, but even if Philip trusts you, I don't."

A SHARP RAP sounded on the rear door of the van.

Jamal checked the sideview mirror. "It's The Man's car. A couple of his goons are riding shotgun."

"Let him in," Yu ordered.

Jamal hopped out of the driver's seat and moved to the rear of the van. From outside, he unlocked the doors and opened both.

Vince looked up, through his own blood, and locked gazes with David Kovner. He wished Yu hadn't tied his hands behind his back. Vince would like nothing more than to hurl himself at the bastard, taking him down to the ground where a snake like him belonged.

He wondered somewhere in the back of his mind if Lucas and Casey would figure out what had happened. If someone had gotten a line on the van and would be coming to stop this tragedy. But he was sorely afraid that wasn't going to happen. His ability to look on the bright side of things had considerably dimmed in the last few minutes. Maybe the CIA could still pinpoint Kat's position if what he'd heard about their tracking techniques was true.

Kat obviously still thought she was one of them and was going to be instrumental in dozens of deaths.

In addition, once his hands had been tied, Yu had beaten him unmercifully. Not that he couldn't take it, he could and had. But now, he was pretty much worthless, mentally—if not entirely physically.

Kat was lost to him.

He'd failed at his mission.

And people were going to die because of it.

Kovner stepped into the van. His two gorillas remained outside, near his car, keeping watch.

"So, this is our spy," he said, sounding as much like an American as Vince. Kovner crouched and made a show of studying Vince. "I would be very interested in knowing which organization sent you. I am certain it was not the CIA. They have failed to infiltrate our organization for too long."

Vince didn't say a word.

"Answer him," Yu commanded, raising his hand again.

"I'll tell you who sent me," Vince said, his voice broken. He was pretty sure he had another cracked rib or two. He took a shallow breath, wincing with the piercing pain.

Kovner leaned forward slightly. "I'm waiting."

Vince spat in his face.

That cost him.

By the time Yu was finished with him, Vince couldn't sit up. He lay on his side, his arms aching from being pulled so tightly behind him. His whole body throbbed.

"Enough." Kovner's voice. "The chapel is filling now," he said, gesturing to the monitor Jamal had stationed between the two seats.

Vince curled, grunting with the effort, so that he could see the monitor. Couples and families filled the pews. Vince wanted to rant at Yu and Kovner...wanted to make them see how wrong this was.

"Wait," Yu said suddenly.

Vince glanced over at him, Yu was staring at his watch again. Vince's heart shuddered to a stop.

Yu counted down, "Three, two, one. *Boom!*" He smiled down at Vince. "No more shop." His smile widened. "No more Callahan."

Vince hoisted himself back into a sitting position,

anger numbing the new pain. "I'll get you. In hell if that's what it takes."

When Yu would have pummeled him again, Kovner held up a hand. "The priest is moving into position."

Nausea roiled in Vince's gut as he watched the priest move up to stand in front of the tabernacle.

"Five minutes," Jamal announced. He glanced out the window. "Leva and Kat should have been back by now."

Yu jerked his head toward the door. "Check it out."

Kovner turned his attention back to Vince. "No one can stop us, Mr. Ferrelli. Not the CIA, not your people. No one. Because we don't leave a trail. Our people are prepared to die for their cause. We recruit, we strike and then we disappear." Kovner shrugged. "The strategy is perfect."

Vince nodded. "I know exactly what you mean, but does your boy here know it?" He inclined his head in Yu's direction. "Does he really understand he's about to make the ultimate sacrifice for the cause?"

Anger glinted in Kovner's eyes. "Philip is very important to us. I have no idea what you are insinuating."

"Think about it, Yu," Vince urged. "Who else but you survived the one other mission you've been in? Who gave you the order to eliminate Will?"

"Is everything all right, Mr. Kovner?" the smaller of the two gorillas asked as he climbed into the driver's seat of the van.

Yu's uncertain gaze cut to the newcomer, then back to Vince. "WSA needs me. I have not failed them as Will did. He lacked focus and discipline."

"Precisely, Philip," Kovner agreed.

Vince laughed, then coughed. His ribs hurt like hell. "You just keep telling yourself that, *Philip*." He mocked Kovner.

"This is only the beginning, Mr. Ferrelli," Kovner told him, needing or wanting the moment to brag. "We have many more plans. Plans you can't even begin to imagine."

Jamal rushed up to the back of the van, Leva in tow. "I can't find Kat," he huffed.

"She's lost it," Leva said, looking around as if afraid Kat would pounce on her from out of nowhere. "The bitch tried to kill me and I was only defending—"

Kovner stopped her next words, his attention going back to the monitor. "It's time."

With Kovner's man still in the driver's seat, Jamal climbed into the passenger seat and quickly made a final adjustment to the monitor. Vince looked from Jamal to Leva then back to the monitor. A new rush of fear surged through him. Where the hell was Kat? What if Leva had already killed her? He wiggled his hands, arched his wrists, struggling with his bindings, ignoring the bite into his flesh.

Yu counted down once more. "Ten, nine, eight…"

Vince struggled harder.

"…five, four, three…"

Vince stared at the monitor, blood and emotion blurring his vision, but not so much so that he didn't see all the people who were about to die.

"…one!"

Vince's breath stalled in his lungs.

Nothing happened.

A beat of silence filled the van.

"What is this?" Kovner bellowed.

A smile stretched across Vince's face as he stared at the peaceful scene on the monitor. "Well, I'll be damned."

A hissing *pop* echoed in the front of the van. Jamal slumped against the passenger door.

Yu's eyes went wide. "What are you doing?"

The second round from Kovner's goon silenced Philip Yu. Leva was next, dropping on the asphalt.

As Yu's body collapsed onto its side, Vince couldn't help a twinge of regret. Yu was young…he'd been led down the wrong path—Vince's fury whipped to Kovner—by this maniac.

The gorilla outside hoisted Leva into the van right next to Vince. He scooted away when the goon reached for him.

"Get him in the car," Kovner commanded, then turned to Vince. "You see, Mr. Ferrelli, we plan to keep you alive a little while longer." He gave a little knowing nod. "Just until we determine for whom you work, then we'll put you out of your misery." He placed a hand on Vince's shoulder before he was dragged from the van. "And believe me, it is going to be miserable."

"Freeze!"

Kat.

Tears of relief burned behind Vince's eyes. He'd never been so damned glad to see anyone in his life.

"Kill her!" Kovner commanded, his voice savage. He was not accustomed to failure.

"I wouldn't do that if I were you." A weapon engaged right behind the gorilla nearest Kat.

The large white lettering on the black flack jacket read ATF. Vince almost laughed out loud. The cavalry was here!

The other guy who'd arrived with Kovner was forced away from the van and down against the pavement. "Spread 'em," another ATF agent ordered.

"You had me going there for a little while," Vince said to Kat, too damned glad to see her to care if she was still mad at him or not.

"You told me to come rescue you." She shrugged and lowered her weapon. "What else could I do?"

"You could untie me," Vince suggested, desperate to get his arms around her.

Without warning, Kovner lunged for Kat. Vince dived for Kovner but missed, couldn't catch himself, and landed hard against the asphalt. He grimaced, feeling as if he'd just added another fracture to the growing list, and pushed up as quickly as he could.

"Anybody moves and I'll kill her." Kovner had Kat's gun jammed into her temple.

Vince swore softly. "Let her go," he said hoarsely. "Take me."

By now a whole herd of ATF agents had descended upon their position. Kovner was too smart for them, though. He kept himself shielded by the open van doors and Kat's body. He had no intention of allowing a sniper strike.

Kovner smirked at Vince. "Why don't I just take you

both?" He gestured to one of the agents. "Have him cut you loose and you can drive."

Vince moved to one of the agents and gave him his back as instructed. The quick-thinking agent slid a small handgun into Vince's waistband as he fumbled to release him with the other hand.

Vince stepped forward. "Ready," he said.

Kovner shook his head. "Put your hands up and turn around."

Vince stilled. "Are we going or what? You keep hanging around and one of these guys is going to take—"

"Turn around!"

Slowly, reluctantly, Vince turned around.

Kat cried out in pain.

Vince shook with the effort of maintaining his cool.

"Toss the weapon aside and get in the van."

Exhaling a breath, then drawing in deeply, groping for calm, Vince removed the weapon from his waistband and placed it on the ground, then kicked it away. When he turned around, Kovner was already dragging Kat into the van.

"Close the doors," he instructed her.

His arm still crooked around her neck, she reached forward and did as she was told.

Vince got behind the wheel and started the engine. "Where are we going?"

"Just get out of here," Kovner roared.

Vince backed up, then pulled forward through the throng of black-suited personnel. He caught a glimpse of a couple of Specialists in the group. It wasn't until that moment that he remembered…

Callahan.

"Turn right," Kovner instructed when Vince stopped where the parking lot met the street.

Forcing away thoughts of Callahan for the moment, Vince looked left then right. He blinked. He'd forgotten about Jamal. He still lay slumped against the passenger door.

Vince needed a plan. When they got where they were going, Vince would take Kovner. It was simple. Even if it cost him his life, no one else Vince cared about was going to die today.

Then it hit him.

…keep an extra weapon taped under the dash when I'm driving.

Vince leaned fully back and covertly glanced downward. Sure enough, there was a 9 mm taped under the dash. He glanced at Jamal and silently thanked him.

The light at the intersection turned red and Vince stopped.

"Which way?" he asked. He looked back at Kovner for the answer.

"Straight."

Kovner still had one arm around Kat, but she had pulled away from him as best she could. The two bodies were sprawled only inches away.

"Then what?" Vince wanted to know, stalling for time.

"Shut up and drive!" Kovner's dark face was crimson with rage.

Kat's gaze collided with Vince's for one fleeting moment.

And that was all it took.

She knew what to do.

"Okay, okay," Vince said, disgusted. "We have to wait for the light to turn green since there are cars in front of us. And you need a plan. You can't expect to escape without a plan. Those guys are bound to be close behind us."

With that said, Vince jerked the gun from under the dash and swung it toward Kovner. Kat had drawn as far away from him as physically possible. Momentarily distracted by the prospect that the authorities were following them, Kovner never knew what hit him. He toppled onto Philip Yu.

Vince drove the van onto the sidewalk to his right and jumped out. He jerked the rear doors open and pulled Kat into his arms.

For a long time he couldn't say anything. He could only hold her, liquid emotion slipping past his clenched lids. But he didn't care. She was safe.

He finally pulled back and looked down at her. "You're okay? You're really okay? I thought I'd lost you when Leva showed up with Jamal and not you."

One coppery eyebrow quirked upward. "Leva and I had a sort of parting of ways. She tried to kill me, I sent her to nappy town." Kat shrugged it off in typical Kat fashion. "Obviously it didn't last as long as I'd hoped. Too bad she woke up and went running back to Kovner."

Vince searched Kat's face, scarcely hearing her words. "Your memory is functioning normally? You know where you are, what's going on and all that?"

She laughed. "Yes to all of it." She wiped the tears

from her cheeks. "The last couple of days it had been coming back in bits and pieces, but then sometime during the night..." She shrugged. "I don't know if it was the dreams or what." Her gaze sought his. "But I remembered everything."

Vince plowed his fingers through his hair and exhaled a mighty breath. "Thank God." He went still. "Callahan." The name was scarcely a whisper. "They—"

"Callahan's fine," Kat assured him. Her green eyes tender with emotions.

Vince frowned. "How do you know?"

The squeal of tires echoed around them as a dozen or so official but unmarked vehicles skidded to a stop.

"How did they know where to come?" Vince glanced at the entourage.

Kat smiled. "Give me some credit here, Ferrelli. After Philip Yu left me with no other option except to give you up, I had to devise a backup plan. I left a note in the SUV with the decoys. And I disarmed the bomb in the basement just like I did the ones in the chapel." When he started to interrupt, she went on. "But just in case Leva had left any other surprises, I told them in the note to get a bomb squad to the house, specifically to the basement."

Thank God. That meant that Callahan was not only safe, but that she hadn't been trapped in the dark for too long. Those light sticks only lasted for a few hours.

"You're something, you know that, Kat?" He wanted to pull her into his arms again. "I've missed you...and then some."

Her smile faded instantly. "We need to talk."

This was it. The honeymoon was over. She knew what he'd done to her and she hadn't forgiven him yet. He couldn't blame her. He nodded. "Yeah, we do."

Pain streaked across her face. She gasped and grabbed her head with both hands. "Oh, God!" she cried.

Vince caught her just before she hit the ground. "Get me an ambulance," he shouted to anyone listening.

He cradled Kat against his chest and tried to comfort her. "It's okay, baby. It's going to be okay."

It had to be.

After all they'd been through, anything less was unacceptable.

"HOW LONG does this take?" Vince paced the waiting room yet again. He didn't know how much more of the waiting he could endure. The pain from his numerous injuries had faded into insignificance.

Lucas pointed his cane at him. "You're working yourself up for nothing, Ferrelli. She's going to be fine. Now sit down, that's an order."

Vince shook his head and dropped into the closest chair. Only Lucas Camp could announce with complete confidence and authority, as if he had the Almighty in his hip pocket, that Kat was going to be fine.

When several seconds had passed, Lucas said, "You did good, Ferrelli. The two goons who accompanied Kovner have spilled their guts. The CIA has people en route to dismantle WSA as we speak."

Vince nodded. "Good." It was good, but Vince's heart wasn't in the conversation. He needed to know about Kat. He'd forced the ambulance driver to patch a call through to Damrus's cell phone. Damrus had met them at the hospital. Vince hoped like hell he could straighten out this mess.

As uncertain as everything was, the one thing that he was sure of was that he couldn't live the rest of his life without Kat.

"The ATF boys took care of the disarmed devices at the chapel as well as at the Port Charlotte house." Lucas propped both hands on his cane. "This is a major hurdle in homeland security." He looked Vince straight in the eyes. "This country is a safer place because of men like you, Ferrelli. I know the price is often high, but it's worth it when you weigh the alternatives."

Vince nodded. A kind of numbness had set in. But he knew Lucas Camp spoke from personal experience.

"Any word?"

Vince looked up to find Callahan strolling into the lobby. He pushed to his feet, as did Lucas.

"Nothing yet. Sure glad to see you," Vince murmured as he pulled her close. "I thought you were a goner there for a little while."

She pulled back. "So did I." The look she gave him was telling.

Vince knew what she meant. "You're one tough cookie, Blue."

She hugged him again, then turned to Lucas. "I understand you wanted to see me."

He clapped her on the shoulder. "As I told Ferrelli, you did good, Callahan. Top-notch work."

She nodded. "Thank you, sir."

"Right now," Lucas went on. "I'd like you to get on back home and get a couple days' rest. We've got an important mission for you. One that can't wait more than forty-eight hours."

Callahan stiffened her spine and lifted her chin. "I'll be ready in twenty-four, sir."

"That's what I'd hoped to hear." He nodded approvingly. Lucas resumed his seat and his vigil for word on Kat.

Callahan nodded toward the bank of elevators. Vince took the hint and walked with her in that direction.

"Thanks, Ferrelli, for keeping my secret," she said, her eyes downcast.

He stabbed the call button and draped one arm over her shoulder and squeezed. "It's okay, Callahan. We all have our secret weaknesses."

She looked up at him and scoffed. "I'll bet you don't have one."

He bent and whispered into her ear, sharing with her the one thing that scared him to death.

She nodded. "Guess you do." The elevator doors slid open and she stepped inside. "See you around, Ferrelli." She wiggled her fingers in a little wave.

Vince waved back, not turning away until the doors swished closed again. He trudged back to the waiting room, his heart somewhere in the proximity of his feet. Kat had to get through this. There were things he needed to say to her.

He blinked furiously and dropped back into the seat Lucas had ordered him to take earlier. He had to make this right. Even if she never forgave him, he had to try.

The double doors leading to the operating room suddenly burst open. A frazzled Dr. Damrus appeared.

Vince was on his feet and rushing to meet Damrus before the doors closed behind him. Lucas was hot on his heels.

"How is she?" Vince demanded, not wanting to beat around the bush.

Damrus took a breath, released it. Vince gritted his teeth, prepared himself for the worst.

"She came through the procedure with flying colors. There were no outward signs of damage. The CT scan was clean. Everything looks excellent. There's no reason to doubt a full recovery."

There was a "but" in there someplace. "But," Vince prompted.

Damrus looked downtrodden. "We won't know for sure until she is awake and we can question her."

Hope wilted. More waiting.

"She's on her way to recovery now." Damrus tugged Vince slightly aside and whispered, "If you promise to keep my secret about being in Port Charlotte, I'll let you go in and sit with her."

"Deal."

Lucas eyed them both suspiciously. Vince just smiled. He was very good at keeping secrets.

HER MOUTH felt incredibly dry when she woke up.

Kat surveyed the room through blurry eyes. Where

was she? The hospital. Oh, yeah. She vaguely remembered the ride in the ambulance, Vince hovering over her, tears in his eyes.

Kat stilled. After all this time, could she possibly mean that much to him?

She blinked back a wave of moisture. She remembered distinctly him asking her to remember that he'd realized how wrong he'd been…he didn't want her to forget that one thing no matter what. She also remembered vividly the way he'd made love to her. The whispered words…the touch that promised so much.

In four years she'd never for one moment forgotten Vince. She'd been angry for a long time, bitter even, but she'd never once stopped loving him. Still, a part of her wanted to kick his butt for not sticking up for her. Not that it would have made any difference, the outcome would have been the same. But she'd wanted desperately to know that he believed in her and was willing to shout it to all. He'd tried to explain his side of things, but she had refused to listen. She'd seen the regret in his eyes even then, but she'd been too angry and hurt to understand that Vince was only human and susceptible to mistakes the same as she was.

The mission and the implant had to be the explanations for his sudden presence in her life again. She tried to think how that had happened. She remembered volunteering for the program. She wasn't married and didn't have any children. When she'd filled out the questionnaire on her Romeo, she hadn't meant to use Vince…but once she'd filled in all the blanks it was him.

She couldn't make herself undo it. He was, after all, the man who owned her heart—despite their turbulent past. Besides, she'd never really thought the implant would work. She definitely hadn't anticipated it working when she didn't need it to. The implant had kicked in on its own, smack-dab in the middle of the mission. Thank God, Vince had been available and willing to rescue her.

She looked around a little more, trying to get her bearings, and her gaze landed on the man who'd occupied a good many of her thoughts and all of her dreams for more than four years.

Kat smiled. God, he looked good. For a man who'd broken her heart.

A new bandage covered the wound above his right eye. She frowned at the memory of Philip working him over. His chin was beard shadowed and his hair was mussed. His clothes looked slept in…but other than that… He looked like heaven on earth.

She'd gotten over, pretty much anyway, the mistake he'd made. The truth was, she'd made one, too. Despite his plea that she hear him out…that she forgive him for the mistake he'd admitted making, her pride had ruled her emotions. She'd walked away from more than her Navy career, she'd walked away from the only man she'd ever loved without giving him a chance to make things right.

Things would be different now.

Dark lashes fluttered open, revealing his incredible gray eyes. Her heart stopped right then and there. She was certain the monitor tracking her vitals would sound an alert at the nurse's station any moment.

"You're back," he whispered. He stood and moved to her side. "Damn, I'm glad to see that smile."

Kat touched her mouth. She hadn't been aware she was smiling. A shaft of pain slid through her. "My head hurts."

"The implant is gone," Vince told her. "Damrus says everything looks fine. What's your name?"

She frowned. "What?"

Vince cocked a dark eyebrow. "I'm supposed to make sure everything is in working order. So, what's your name?"

She heaved an impatient sigh, frustrated. "Trust me, Ferrelli, everything is in perfect order."

He nodded uncertainly. "Good."

She raked her teeth across her bottom lip. How could he look so good? How could she want him so badly and still feel inclined to kick his butt? "How about you?" she asked grudgingly, petulantly. "You okay?"

He pressed a hand to his abdomen. "Only two fractured ribs. My shoulder hurts like hell and my head still aches, but, otherwise, I'm good to go."

To her irritation, another smile tugged its way across her mouth. She immediately dispatched it. "There's just one thing that still bothers me."

Worry captured his expression once more. "What? Do I need to call a doctor or nurse?"

She almost shook her head, but caught herself just in time. She crooked her finger. "Come closer."

He leaned down, escalating concern marring his brow.

"Ever since I fully regained my memory the only thing I could think about was kicking your butt." She narrowed her gaze at him. "So I avoided talking to you or even looking at you as much as possible. I didn't want to blow our cover. The one thing that kept me going was the knowledge that in the end I'd have my revenge."

He looked startled. "I, uh, can understand that," he said honestly, his gaze telegraphing the sincerity of it. "I was wrong. I should have stood up for you in BUDS training, but I didn't. And I lost you because of it." He took her hand in his, studying the IV taped there. "Losing you again was the one thing that scared me to death. Still does."

"Here's the deal," she said succinctly. "I won't kick your butt with you in the condition you're in, okay? You took two beatings on my account as it is, so we'll call it even." She quirked an eyebrow. "Lucky you."

"Kat, I don't expect you—"

She waved off the rest of his words. "I'm too exhausted to discuss this at length or to argue about what was whose fault and who owes who what, but I forgive you, okay?"

He looked even more startled than before. "I would understand if you didn't."

"But I do." She squeezed his fingers and smiled. "What you did was wrong. Walking away without giving you a chance to make it right was wrong of me. When you love someone, it's supposed to conquer all. I didn't give us a chance."

He stilled. "You love me?"

"Like you didn't know," she teased playfully.

He shrugged, a grin twitching his lips. "I sure was hoping I wasn't in this boat alone."

She turned serious then, her heart bursting with the knowledge that he loved her, too. "I want us to try again. Are you game?"

"Oh, yeah." He pressed his lips to her forehead. "Anytime, baby." He straightened and looked at her suspiciously. "Just one question. What all did you put in that Romeo profile? Lucas said—"

"That information is on a need-to-know basis only," she interrupted smoothly. "Now kiss me, Ferrelli, before I change my mind about kicking your butt."

"Happy to oblige, ma'am."

He kissed her. And in that moment when heat and desire and need and plain old lust merged as one deep in her heart she knew without a single doubt that she and Ferrelli were about to rewrite history.

Mission Briefing

Lucas Camp didn't like the way Mission Recovery's esteemed director planned to handle this next assignment. Admittedly, Lucas respected Thomas Casey and trusted his judgment without reservation, but this one was personal. And personal was never good when it came to a mission.

"Edgar Rothman is my friend," Casey said at last. His piercing gaze settled on Lucas. "I won't insult your intelligence by pretending otherwise. He blames himself for what happened to Major Drake."

Lucas sighed and again scanned the meager contents of the file on Noah Drake. "They sure aren't giving us much." *They* being the little brother that Big Brother insisted didn't exist.

"No." Casey folded his arms on his desk and leaned forward. "But you, better than anyone, understand that level of necessary security."

Security was one thing, Lucas mused. But this was something else altogether. This secret little group—

little being the operative word—went way beyond simple security measures. The group didn't even have a name. They were simply known as "The Others."

Extensive research and development, that was their game. That's what Lucas did know about the group, he deliberately refused to call them "The Others." It went against his grain, made him want to gnash his teeth.

"According to this file," Lucas said out loud, knowing full well Casey already knew the details better than he did, "Major Drake took part in a mission five years ago that brought down a high-level ring of traitors inside our own government." Lucas remembered the incident well. "In order to accomplish his mission he participated in a *chameleon* experiment that resulted in dire side effects."

Casey nodded. "Bright light of any sort would be the death of him. He has no choice but to exist in near darkness."

"And we're not supposed to ask what this *chameleon* business means?" Lucas wasn't even sure he wanted to know.

"That's right."

Lucas closed the file and shook his head. "The leader of the group Drake brought down is out of prison now." It wasn't a question. Due to a piece of crucial evidence having gone missing, General Regan Bonner had gotten off with a slap on the hand. Now he was free to exact the revenge he'd sworn he would have against Drake. This all according to Rothman, the man who created the technology that got Noah Drake into this predicament in the first place.

"We have no actual proof that Bonner is involved with the threatening letters Drake has been receiving, but that would be my first guess."

Lucas agreed. "So we're sending in Blue."

Casey nodded. "Drake doesn't want any protection. In fact, he doesn't want anything from anyone even remotely associated with the government. He just wants to be left alone."

Lucas cocked an eyebrow. "A little bitter, is he?"

"A little," Casey allowed with a twitch of his lips that might have been an attempt at a smile. "So we're going to have to go in the back door on this one. We're sending in Callahan to keep him off guard, while I carry the outfield."

Lucas didn't like this. "You shouldn't take that kind of risk. You're—"

"The decision is made," Casey cut him off. "This is personal and I intend to take care of it personally."

Oh, Lucas was very much aware of that.

"I'll go," he said resolutely. "I need a break from the office and I have some personal business to attend to." Casey didn't need to know the details. "You're needed here."

Casey looked him square in the eye and said, "Leberman?"

To say Lucas was stunned would be a tremendous understatement.

Casey smirked just a little. "I know more than you think. You've been meeting with a representative from the Colby agency. Does Victoria know?"

Lucas tamped down the irritation that rose instantly. "I can handle the Leberman situation." He didn't have to say what was actually on his mind. Casey could read it in his expression: Mind your own business.

"And you want me to stay clear of personal assignments?" Casey quipped.

"You're the director," Lucas reminded. "I am more expendable than you."

"That's a matter of opinion."

Lucas nodded, conceding the point.

Casey steepled his fingers and thought about the situation for a moment.

"Callahan will be more receptive to my involvement," Lucas interjected knowing the comment wouldn't go down easy, but it was true. Casey remained untouchable…the troops had noticed.

"All right," Casey allowed. "But if you need me—"

"I won't," Lucas assured him.

"Drake won't be easy to deal with."

A grin tugged at the corners of Lucas's mouth. "You're counting on Callahan's being able to keep Drake off guard since she's a woman."

Casey smiled this time, a knowing gesture that lacked real amusement. "From all accounts it's been five years since he's been with a woman. And since he's physically able and fit, there's every reason to believe he would still respond to one."

Lucas chuckled. "Well, knowing Callahan like I do, I wish the guy luck. Callahan knows her business. She won't let anything happen to Noah Drake, but if he makes a pass at her, she might just kick his butt. I'm hoping that old fire will kick in and make him more receptive."

"I'm counting on that. According to Rothman, Drake never could resist a challenge."

Lucas didn't know which one to waste his sympathy on, Drake or Callahan. One thing was certain, his Specialists were all trained well. If it took charm or even seduction to make Noah Drake pliable, Specialist Blue Callahan could handle the job. The time away from the office would give Lucas the opportunity to put his own ghosts to rest as well.

Lucas pushed to his feet, using his cane for support. "I'll brief Callahan."

"Lucas," Casey said, waylaying him when he would have turned away. "You are *not* expendable. Keep that in mind."

Lucas smiled. "You're the boss."

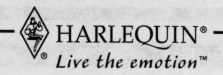

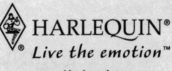

HARLEQUIN®
INTRIGUE®

BREATHTAKING ROMANTIC SUSPENSE

Shared dangers and passions lead to electrifying romance and heart-stopping suspense!

Every month, you'll meet six new heroes who are guaranteed to make your spine tingle and your pulse pound. With them you'll enter into the exciting world of Harlequin Intrigue— where your life is on the line and so is your heart!

THAT'S INTRIGUE—
ROMANTIC SUSPENSE
AT ITS BEST!

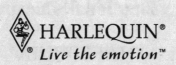

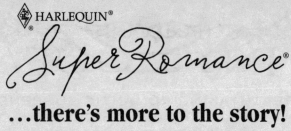

HARLEQUIN®

Super Romance®

...there's more to the story!

Superromance.
A *big* satisfying read about unforgettable
characters. Each month we offer *six* very different
stories that range from family drama to adventure
and mystery, from highly emotional stories to
romantic comedies—and much more! Stories
about people you'll believe in and care about.
Stories too compelling to put down....

Our authors are among today's *best* romance
writers. You'll find familiar names and talented
newcomers. Many of them are award winners—
and you'll see why!

If you want the biggest and best
in romance fiction, you'll get it
from Superromance!

Exciting, Emotional, Unexpected...

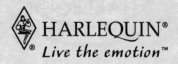

HARLEQUIN®
Live the emotion™

Harlequin® Historical
Historical Romantic Adventure!

Imagine a time of chivalrous knights and unconventional ladies, roguish rakes and impetuous heiresses, rugged cowboys and spirited frontierswomen— these rich and vivid tales will capture your imagination!

Harlequin Historical . . . they're too good to miss!

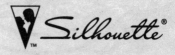

SPECIAL EDITION™

Emotional, compelling stories that capture the intensity of living, loving and creating a family in today's world.

Modern, passionate reads that are powerful and provocative.

nocturne

Dramatic and sensual tales of paranormal romance.

Romances that are sparked by danger and fueled by passion.